THE GIRL IN THE HALO

A Novel

By

Alan L. Nobler

Jeff —
Thanks again
for your help!
Alan

"The Girl in the Halo" illuminates the poorly understood problems associated with domestic violence experienced daily by family law attorneys and victims. It vividly depicts the frustrations faced by those involved in the legal system. While it should be required reading for law students and judges, it is a compelling read for anyone interested in this important societal problem. It's a wonderful book.

Garrett C. Dailey, CFLS, AAML, IAFL, ACFTL
Author & publisher of Attorney's BriefCase®
Family Law Research software

When I read this book, it reminded me of my years sitting on the bench. The case the author describes is special, but it is also typical. This story is played out every day in our family courts. The dynamics of domestic violence are well known and this story exemplifies those dynamics very effectively.

In fact, it is a book I could not put down. Will she change her mind and go back to her husband/abuser? Will she be able to testify in court? Will she be able to regain custody of her child?

And what about the attorney representing her? Will he succeed? Will he ever get paid? Will the professionals he has consulted be paid?

There are so many different aspects to this case and the book explores them thoroughly. I strongly recommend that you read it. You won't be disappointed.

Judge Leonard Edwards
Former Superior Court Judge, Santa Clara County, California
Judge-in-Residence, Center for Families, Children & the Courts

Reads like a powerful legal thriller...captures the role of money and legal maneuvering, including the pitfalls of representing an aggrieved victim. I enjoyed reading this in one session.

Lilly Grenz, LCSW
Former Director of Santa Clara County Family Court Services

"The Girl with the Halo" takes an intolerable topic and makes it not only tolerable, but compelling with its fast-paced, insightful, poignant and sometimes funny telling. An important *"must read."*

Ann Ravel

Former Santa Clara County Counsel,
Deputy Assistant Attorney General for Torts & Consumer Litigation
in the Civil Division of the U.S. Dept of Justice,
and Commissioner of the Federal Election Commission

A minority of domestic violence survivors involved in Family Court child custody litigation are fortunate enough to have the kind of legal representation and informed victim advocacy like that provided by attorney and his colleagues in Alan Nobler's "The Girl in the Halo."

While the Courts are better informed and laws are more responsive to domestic violence issues than in the mid-1980s when the book is set, the traumatic impact of domestic violence on its victims, including children exposed to such abuse, continues to be minimized and discounted. Family Law judges, attorneys, and involved mental health professionals across the country typically receive little training on the dynamics of domestic violence and trauma-informed responses to litigants. Without such training the legal system itself can be inadvertently coopted into enabling the offender's continued abuse of power and control over the victim-survivor.

Kudos to the author for shining a light on a problem which, over the course of a lifetime, along with rape and/or stalking, effects more than 1 in 3 women and 1 in 4 men in the United States.

Steve Baron, MA, LMFT (ret.)

Santa Clara County Domestic Violence Death Review Team
Former Director of Santa Clara County Family Court Services

People, especially women, going through a dysfunctional marriage often feel helpless and our legal system too often fails them. While a work of fiction, this page-turner reads like a true story, as it engulfs the reader into the psychology and reasons why people get trapped in violent relationships.

Written for the general public to learn the dynamics between attorneys, their clients, and the courts, I would also recommend it for legal professionals to understand what dilemmas many people face coping with failed relationships in real life. Attorneys who do not practice family law will learn that Carol's story is not an isolated one, and this book should be mandatory reading for all new attorneys that are going into family law.

It's a stunning portrayal of our chaotic legal labyrinth, and should awaken the powers to be to consider what more can be done to help these victims.

Hal D. Bartholomew, CFLS, AAML
Bartholomew & Wasznicky LLP, Sacramento
Former President & co-founder of Collaborative Practice California

A fast-paced, easy-to-read book that explained facets of the legal system I've not seen on TV or in other books. Its description of family dynamics and the cycle of domestic abuse is accurate and well presented. I enjoyed the character of Dr. Gold and the way she related to both her client and the lawyer.

Rocki Kramer, LCSW
Founder & Former Executive Director
Almaden Valley Counseling Service

a PennedSource Production

Dedication

First, to my wife, Barbara, who kept me grounded during my years of practice and in writing this book. Fifty-six years and counting.

Second, to the many victims of spousal abuse, both women and men, I worked with during my forty-eight years practicing law in Santa Clara County, California.

CONTENTS

THE GIRL IN THE HALO

Prologue

February 9, 1985

Carol trembled, lying naked under the sheets, the way Bill wanted to find her whenever he stumbled home late at night. Despite her bared skin, Carol was not shivering from the unusually blustery cold of the early morning hour; rather, it was the chill of what she knew was about to happen to her. Five days until Valentine's Day and he was out drinking with "his boys" on a Saturday night.

The minutes ticked by. Her fears turned to dread. She cried quietly into her pillow to keep from disturbing 18-month-old Joey, asleep in the next room. She heard the front door click open, counted Bill's stumbling footsteps coming to their bedroom, listened to him kick off his shoes, unbuckle his belt, drop his pants, finish stripping and climb into bed beside her.

Carol anticipated he would be rough with her, as usual whenever he had been drinking, but she flinched at his unexpected movements behind her. With a swift jerk, he slipped his arms under hers, forcing her shoulders back, and gripped her skull with his hands behind her head in a full-Nelson headlock. He had demonstrated that position to her before, when he'd bragged about the indefensible hold he learned on his high-school wrestling team. But tonight it wasn't just for show. It was different. He continued increasing the pressure, forcing her head forward.

Helpless in his grasp, alarmed by his silent power, immediately her mind raced to how she could protect herself. Nothing. He'd never been this brutal before.

"Stop!" she screamed, no longer caring if she woke Joey.

Bill shifted and instead angled her head forward even more.

Carol heard the bones in her spine crunch. A stab of pain shot across her neck.

Sobbing, not daring to struggle against his grip, she begged Bill to release her so she could pee first and get some lubricant. Bill relaxed his hold with a grunt of reluctance and fell back against the pillows, arm across his eyes.

Carol scrambled from the bed and walked slowly into the hall. Suppressing a moan, she stumbled from the house and across the street to Jill's home. She pounded on the door, praying for it to open quickly.

"Carol, dammit, you come home, *now!*" Bill bellowed, his voice carrying in the hushed quiet, his bare feet smacking the front porch steps, charging after her.

Jill's door opened a crack, then all the way open. Jill stood with her bathrobe clutched in her fist, mouth agape. Looking over Carol's nude shoulder, Jill screamed and pulled Carol inside, locked the door, and called the police.

1 - The Collins Case

July 4, 2016

Everybody had gathered at our house in San Jose to have a semi-traditional Fourth of July BBQ. By everybody, I mean three generations of the Gregory and Cramer families. My eldest grandson, Harris, had come into the garage with me to load up the cooler with cold beer. We each took a handle to head back to the pool with our haul when he stopped me.

"Grandpa," he said, "I've got a decision to make about what to study when I go away to college next year." At 17, he had just finished his junior year in high school. His light brown hair fell almost down to his shoulders, still tangled from the pool. A sweet smile got him almost anything he ever wanted, always at the ready, coupled with hazel eyes and a hint of a lisp that was as disarming as his smile. He had good grades and, already an inch taller than my five feet, ten inches, was really into sports.

"What are you interested in?" I wished Harris' dad, Aaron, had asked me for this kind of advice when he was this age.

"Nothing really grabs me for a career. Dad says I should interview all my grandparents about their professions to see if anything they have done inspires me."

"What have you found so far?"

"I wanted to do this with you, first," he said, turning his signature smile at me.

How could you not love this kid? "Well, let's get this beer delivered before they send out a search party, then find a place in the shade to talk." It was 95 degrees out and the pool was full of bodies.

We set the cooler in the shade of the house and each grabbed a bottle.

"We're going to relax in the corner," I called out. Nods and thumbs-up acknowledged us. As we settled in, I said, "OK, Harris. It's your interview. What do you want to know?"

He reached into his pocket and took out a folded piece of paper. I saw he'd written out a list of questions. Good for you, I thought, but instead of telling him, I just waited.

"First," he started, "I'd like to know what was it that made you decide to become a lawyer."

I didn't even have to think. "The war in Viet Nam."

He looked surprised. "We studied that. What did that have to do with you? Were you in the war?"

"When I graduated from college in 1964, we had a military draft in place to get soldiers for the war. I didn't want to go. I realized I had two choices: enlist in a branch of the military that might not get sent to Viet Nam or go to graduate school. There were deferments—postponements—available to graduate students. There were also exceptions for married men. So, I doubled down, asked Grandma Sarah to marry me and also enrolled in law school."

"How did you pick law school?"

"My degree was in business. I thought about an MBA—a Master's in Business Administration—but that was only two years and law school took three. So, I did the math and went to law school at Santa Clara University."

"And that's where you met Uncle Marty?"

I smiled. "Yes. We were the only two Jews in our class at a Catholic University. We bonded and have been friends ever since."

Marty Cramer grew up in the Boyle Heights section of Los Angeles. He was a decent student, but a star on the basketball court. Blonde, six feet, four inches, he had won a full scholarship to Stanford, starting on the varsity team as a sophomore. Late in that season, Marty blew out his knee and never regained the speed and agility he needed to play at that level, so he studied like crazy. Santa Clara University Law School offered him an academic scholarship; he was already exempt from the military draft as 4F due to his knee injury.

We were drawn together by our love of basketball. I had played on my high school team, and was still good enough, when paired with Marty, to dominate the pick-up games around the school and, later, after we were in law practice, at the local YMCA whenever we could break away from our respective offices. It gave us a sense of teamwork that cemented our relationship. It also was a way for us to concentrate on the basic geometry of a game and get our heads out of the convoluted problems facing us in practice. Win or lose, we always came back more relaxed than when we started.

Marty was a born crowd-pleaser. Juries loved him. Just listening to his deep baritone seemed to win people over to him regardless of the argument he was presenting. He could have gone with any of the big trial firms in town, but after five years working at our respective firms, we formed Cramer& Gregory in 1974. It was a true 50-50 partnership, a rarity among lawyers.

Harris peeked at his list of questions. "Was it fun, you know, being a lawyer?"

"Sometimes," I said. "But mostly it was hard work. Looking back, I can't think of anything else I could have done that would have been more gratifying, even if I'd gone into business the way I'd originally planned. For me, it was all about working with people, one on one; helping them solve problems they couldn't solve by themselves."

"What was your most interesting case?"

"The Collins case," I said. "But we won't have time to talk about it now. I see your Grandma Sarah coming over here, and I think that means it's time to start the BBQ."

Sarah, petite and trim, with short brown hair—only her hairdresser knows its real color—waved at us. I know she was happy that Harris and I were having a real conversation and not horsing around doing something that would wind up with me, once again, needing a trip to the emergency room.

"What are you guys so deep in conversation about?" she asked with a smile.

"Grandpa was just about to tell me about the Collins case," Harris said, with a sly grin.

She laughed. "That will take hours, maybe days. It's time to get social, Steve. We have a large crowd to feed."

"Harris," I said, getting up. "Grandma's right. When can you come over and spend the day?"

He pulled out his phone and stared at the screen. "Well," he said, "today's Monday. I'm working for Uncle Alex on Tuesday, so ..." He scrolled through the entries. "How's Friday?"

Uncle Alex was Marty's son. He owned three McDonald's franchises in town and all of the kids seemed to get their first jobs with him. It was a great way to introduce them to the workforce and convince them to go to college. 'Hamburger U,' *the McDonald's training school in Chicago, wasn't our first choice, even though McDonald's had made Alex wealthy.*

We agreed to continue the conversation over breakfast that coming Friday, and returned to the party. Harris jumped into the pool and I headed to the barbeque, clasping and swinging Sarah's hand. I pushed the haunting memories of the Collins case to the back of my mind, again, relying on my lifelong partnership with this wonderful woman to keep me grounded over the coming days.

* * * * *

After our breakfast that Friday morning, Harris joined me to walk Sasha, our six-year-old Golden Retriever. As we set out, Harris asked, "What made this case stand out from all the other cases?"

"Let's start the story and then you can tell me."

2 - The Girl in the Halo

March 27, 1985

The mother and daughter were sitting across the desk from me.

The mother, who I judged to be in her late 50s or early 60s, was dressed in a camel-colored pantsuit, prim, proper, clenching her teeth, clearly stressed. She had on fashionable glasses and overly bright lipstick in a shade of red I couldn't name. My first impression was that she'd had some work done on her face.

Her daughter, late 20s, was introduced as Carol. She was wearing what I immediately recognized as a medical halo. Looking at the contraption, I thought of Rube Goldberg. The metal device encircled her head at the crown of her skull, just above her eyebrows, and connected with four rods anchored from the halo to a vest made of hard plastic with a fleece lining. Two in front, two in back. Four bolts had been drilled directly into her skull attaching the halo. I knew these would ultimately leave scars. Her neck was unnaturally straight.

Carol's long, dark brown hair contrasted starkly to her mother's short cut. I excused her Nike sweatsuit as a product of the difficulties she must have getting into and out of her clothes while wearing the halo. Her eyes were red—I assumed from crying—and she wore no makeup. Both were trim, but not necessarily athletic. There was obvious tension between them. I thought it might be because of the concern her mom had for her daughter's situation and the daughter's shame from having to depend on her mother to get her dressed, cared for, and driven to a lawyer's office.

At first, I assumed Carol was there to file an injury suit for whiplash, but looking down at the intake form I saw this was about a divorce and custody. Belatedly, I recalled Sue whispering that to me when she'd escorted the women into my office.

"This one will be interesting," Sue had said. "Your client is Carol, the young lady in the halo."

Sue Miller had been our first hire at Cramer & Gregory. Tall, slim, almost 40, she'd been my assistant at the old firm and a legal secretary almost 20 years. She knew what she was doing and kept the office running smoothly, with just the right combination of humor and drill sergeant. She was scrupulously thorough, too, and I was confident she had checked for any conflicts in representation, such as if we had been contacted by her husband first, before scheduling the appointment.

My office was pretty typical of many in the building, with light beige walls and a carpet that wouldn't show how much coffee had been spilled on it. The wall behind my large overhang desk had all the ego stuff you expect from professionals: the diploma, certificates from the State Bar of California, the California Supreme Court, a second certificate from the State Bar announcing that I'd passed a test making me a "Family Law Specialist," and some awards from a few other organizations. The only photograph in the room was on my desk facing me, a family portrait of me with Sarah and the kids, Aaron and Mindy. It was there to remind me of what was really important in life. The client chairs were covered in cloth, not leather, which creaks when people squirm, and I chose wooden armrests: sweaty palms enhance wood, but not upholstery. The wall to my right was all window, with a view of the foothills on the east side of San Jose. Across from me hung a large print of Monet's water lilies.

"So, Carol," I asked, "what brings you here today?"

She began by telling me the horrors of her February encounter with her husband that left her in the halo. Weeping, she informed me, "The surgeon said two of my neck vertebrae were crushed and I came within a few millimeters of being a quadriplegic. I'm lucky to even be able to sit here. "

Her mother, Arlene, butted in. "I want you to take that son of a bitch for everything he's worth, and then some! He needs to go to prison for what he did to Carol!" Arlene's anger failed to cause even a wrinkle on her brow.

Wow, I thought. And now it starts.

"How did you get my name?" I asked. Learning the source of a referral was sometimes a way to get an idea about the situation and an opportunity to send an acknowledgement to the referral source.

"My friend, Jill D'Souza, recommended you," Carol answered. "She said you have represented some people she knows. I didn't ask her who they were."

"Well, for my records, I'll put down 'former client.' This situation is as bad as any I've ever heard," I said. "There are a lot of options for us. Can you tell me what happened after the police were called?"

Arlene answered for her daughter. "Carol was inside, at Jill's, waiting for an ambulance. All we know is that the police came, talked to Carol for a few minutes, then went back to her house to talk with Bill when the ambulance came to take Carol to the hospital. Joey stayed with Jill, and Bill was arrested and taken downtown for booking, or whatever."

"Carol, do you know anything else about the criminal proceeding?" I looked at Carol directly, hoping her mother would take the hint. Carol wasn't ready or able to assert herself and Arlene didn't do subtle. She just sat there, shredding a tissue.

Once again, Arlene answered. "We know he has been charged with something and has an attorney, but we don't know any of the other details."

"That's OK, for now. I'll have our investigator follow up on that. What happened to Joey?"

At that point, Carol began crying in earnest. I passed her a box of tissues I kept on the table behind me. She took another tissue, wiped her eyes, and began shredding that one, too.

Arlene gave Carol a look that seemed to me to be contemptuous of Carol's having fallen apart. "Thomas and Mary, Bill's parents, picked him up from Jill and have kept him and won't let us see our grandson at all! Carol has been staying with me. I don't want those bastards to have any time with Joey after the way they raised Bill!"

"I can see how you would feel that way," I replied. "Grandparent custody and visitation is an emerging area in family law. Are you here for me to represent you or Carol?"

"Carol. Arnie and I want her to be with Joey and protected from that abusive son of a bitch."

"All right. If I am going to be representing Carol, there will be things I need to talk to her about that will be covered by attorney-client privilege. That means that only the two of us can be in the room, or any of us could be compelled to tell Bill's attorneys and the court what we talked about. Would it be OK with you if Carol and I have a few minutes together?"

Arlene agreed to go out for a cup of coffee, then asked me if she could use our conference room to call some of her clients while she was waiting. She made a point of telling me she had five houses on active listings, and she was expecting offers to be coming in at any moment. I checked with Sue that the conference room was available and had her set up Arlene in there with a fresh cup of coffee.

With a silent sigh of relief, I closed the door behind Arlene and resumed my seat. I'd been anxious to finally hear something from Carol herself.

"Carol," I asked, "what's going on with you and your mom?"

"What do you mean?" I thought she might be feigning the puzzlement in her response.

"Well, you seemed really uncomfortable when she was answering for you and it looked to me like you were having trouble getting a word in edgewise."

"Um, Mom is really busy, and doesn't have a lot of time for dealing with my problems."

I nodded. "She did seem really concerned about you."

Carol waved her hand dismissively. "That's just her act in the community. The image she wants to build for herself. Me and her haven't been close since even before I started dating Bill a couple of years ago. Then she really went off the rails with me."

"How so?"

"I guess it was because, with all her real estate work, she doesn't have a very good opinion of construction workers. I told her that was what Bill did and she pretty much instantly told me he wasn't good enough for me." She gave a little laugh. "Like I was such a catch. Oh, and when I spent the night with Bill after knowing him a week, she was really pissed. Bill didn't ever do anything to be friendly with her and we kind of drifted apart."

"Drifted apart?"

"I guess that's putting it mildly. I'm an only child and I don't think she ever wanted me. Nothing I ever did was good enough for her. I guess sometime in high school I just stopped trying."

"Was there anything specific that happened in high school that triggered the separation?"

"I think it was the whole thing. Cutting classes to go to the beach in Santa Cruz, Cs and Ds in most of my classes, blowing off curfew and coming home the next morning. I guess it was the whole package."

"What did you do after high school?"

"Mom said that if I wanted to continue living in their house—you know, with her and my dad—I had to go to Junior College and get decent grades. She said she expected a B average. So, I started at San Jose City College with some classes in bonehead English and math and bookkeeping. I did OK, but only had a C+ average so she said I'd have to move out. I'd met a couple of girls at the JC who had an apartment and moved in with them. Dad wouldn't stand up to Mom, but he helped me with the rent and gave me money for my college fees and books."

"How did you cover the rest of your expenses?"

"I found a job at a gas station convenience store. They paid minimum wage, but gave me flexible hours. All the girls pitched in to cover the apartment and food. Once in a while Mom would take me shopping for clothes."

"Are you still in school?"

"No. I dropped out after a year. Then I was working more hours at the gas station for a few years. Then I met Bill and got married. Then I had Joey."

"OK, are you working now?"

"No," she said. "I haven't since Bill hurt me. It's only been about six and a half weeks since my surgery, and the doctor says I can't do any of the things I used to do for another three to five weeks after I'm out of the halo. But I haven't worked since Joey was born anyway."

"How do you manage with the halo?" I tried to imagine what it would be like to be jailed within that contraption and inwardly shuddered.

"I don't. I can't dress or bathe myself. Mom washes my hair twice a week. It's like I'm two, getting a sponge bath. I can't wear anything that doesn't open in the front." She quickly ran her hand down the zipper of her sweatshirt. "And eating! Try eating when you are stuck looking straight ahead! It's hard to drink without a straw. Forget soup. I need a clean bib at every meal. I feel so helpless." She grabbed another tissue. "The first week in this damn thing my arms and shoulders were black and blue from walking into doorways. I'm always sleepy and spend most of my time in a recliner, even at night. You can probably tell I'm cranky a lot."

"How much longer will you have to wear it?"

She smiled. "I'm seeing Dr. Anton tomorrow. If he gives the OK, I can get it off then. If not...I don't know. The target date was eight weeks and it's now almost seven weeks."

Carol continued her story. Only 28 years old at the time of the rape, she'd been living in the house on Vistamont for two years. Their son, Joey, was then 18 months old and giving her a sense of self-worth, something she'd never experienced before. She loved every moment with him—even his teething, tantrums, and dirty diapers. She would give her life for him.

I knew I'd have to get more information, so I concentrated on the statistical information we'd need to fill out the necessary forms. She wanted to file for divorce, gain custody of Joey with child support, and whatever else we could think of. At least she knew there was a restraining order issued as part of the criminal case that kept Bill at least 100 yards away from her.

Worrying that Carol was too distressed to remember many of the coming details of the legal process I needed to share, I then asked Sue to bring Arlene back. I also wanted to check in with Arlene about my fees, since Carol was unemployed. This was not a case I'd want to do pro bono because of the open-ended time and immense energy it would require.

Arlene settled into the chair next to Carol, and I walked them through the process: we would file a Petition for Dissolution of Marriage, a Motion for Temporary Spousal and Child Support, Custody, and Family Law Restraining Orders. We went through the fee contract: I would bill $150 per hour on the Family Court aspects of her case. I couldn't imagine having any difficulty with the custody aspect, and without good information on their income, support was a guess.

About their finances, Carol told me that Bill's job in construction was driving big earth-moving equipment. They didn't know what his income was and didn't have tax returns. She said that Bill's father was a wealthy developer with a lot of power in town; that ultimately, I wouldn't have any trouble collecting my fees from him.

I'd heard that before.

Deliberately meeting each of their gazes, I cleared my throat. "While we hope the judge will award attorney fees, they never seem to award enough to cover the actual fees and costs we will have to charge. So, I'm going to make the contract between us and not dependent on the court award. OK?" After a pause, I asked, "Arlene, will you be willing to guarantee Carol's fees and costs with our office?"

"Absolutely not!" I was surprised by the forcefulness of Arlene's reply. "This is Carol's case. I will loan her the money for a retainer, but I want you both to know that this is a loan and you can't just count on me for more."

That's cold, I thought, and immediately increased the retainer to $5,000.

Arlene wrote me the check, but only after Carol promised Arlene that it was a loan that she would pay back. I assured them that I'd have a draft of the documents for court within a few days and would call them as soon as the papers were ready for signing. Before they left, I asked if Jules Armstrong, our part time investigator, could take a few pictures of Carol secured in the halo.

Carol frowned, appearing reluctant. "I can't stand the way I look right now. Why would I need to do that?"

"That is exactly why," I answered. "You are uncomfortable and embarrassed. I see that as something we will need to show a judge before this is over. I know you will always remember the pain you are in now, but the degree of pain and discomfort should come through in the pictures—perhaps more vividly than through your own words."

She finally agreed, and I sent her off with Jules, confident in his high level of professionalism to capture Carol as a victim as well as put her at ease with the process. Sharp as a tack, he had a way of getting anybody to talk to him, putting together a lot of the accident science for Marty's personal injury cases and handling the bulk of witness interviews. He also helped in some of the divorce cases when we suspected someone was hiding assets. Not like the old days when photos of hubby *in flagrante delicto* made a difference in support and custody cases.

3 - Steve's Misgivings

March 27, 1985

I called for Sue and Marty to come in and talk about what needed to be done. Usually, we don't meet on a case unless there was a problem. This case smelled funny from the start, but I was having trouble figuring out why.

Sue took the information from my intake interview notes to start the Petition and Motions, coffee cup in hand, clearly ready for a case review.

Jules also joined us. He was 35 years old and of medium build, with longish sandy hair and freckles. In his jeans and striped long-sleeved shirt he looked like a laid-back college student. Nobody would spot the black belt karate master behind that facade.

"Marty," I began, "this is either going to be really easy or an absolute pain. Who do you know down at the DA's office that can get us current on the criminal aspect of the case? If you aren't comfortable with this case, I'll drop it before we get too far into the mud."

"Steve, you sound uncertain. What's up?" Marty knew me well.

"I'm having trouble figuring it out myself," I said. "Carol seems so vulnerable and helpless. I've never seen injuries this cruel in a divorce case. We talk about serious injuries caused by car accidents, but not *intentional* stuff like breaking someone's neck. Getting restraining orders for threatening bodily harm, slapping, hitting, and even throwing things at each other is something every divorce lawyer must deal with. This whole situation is nauseating—I want to throw up every time I think about what this girl faced that night. This isn't like TV, you know, impersonal. This is very personal."

Sue nodded her head. "Mindy just turned 15, didn't she? Starting to date soon, I bet. And already telling her Dad she knows what she's doing."

"Yeah, the thought of my daughter getting caught up in a relationship or situation like this just tears at me," I admitted. "But it's more. I'm having trouble visualizing the procedural steps to make everything work. We're not criminal prosecutors, after all. If that isn't enough, holding up my share of the office expenses could be compromised for a while; this could turn into an awful lot of work." I hesitated. "But I confess I'm already more emotionally involved than maybe I should be. There's something about seeing that girl imprisoned in that halo ..." My throat closed up.

Jules nodded, and I spotted a glimmer of moisture in Sue's eyes.

Legal firms are famous for breaking up over perceived inequality between the fees generated by the lawyers and the amounts they took out in draw. Marty and I had a good thing going, sharing finances equally. I didn't want to do anything to lose the second most important partnership in my life. We both took time off for pro bono work at the court, various bar association committees, and charitable organizations. Even short-term legal work for senior citizens—stuff that wouldn't take more than three or four hours at a time. But never a case that could rack up hundreds of hours.

"I hear you, Steve," Marty said. "As it happens, we've just settled the Margoles injury case, so we've got a cushion in the bank. There's a couple more where I've got the insurance companies on the ropes, so don't worry about money. We're covered. You're covered. I've got a couple of guys from the old firm with connections at the DA's. But I'll bet Jules can find out faster than I can. I'll place the calls and should have something by lunchtime tomorrow. So, don't worry about money."

"Marty," I said, "it's not just the money, it's all about the partnership. You don't know how much I appreciate that. Thank you." I'm sure he heard my big sigh because he shot me a huge smile and a thumbs-up. I asked, "Do you know anything about this father-in-law, Thomas Collins? I hear he is some kind of developer. Something of a big shot in San Jose."

Marty shook his head. "Never heard of him. But you know that's not my circle. What do you think, Jules? What do you think we'll have to budget for you on this?"

"Hmm." Jules scratched his head, a sign he was deep in thought. "Let's start with a couple of hours, then take another look at the whole thing. By the way, I think I caught a couple of pictures that will help in any kind of trial. Carol's tragic expressions really show the magnitude of her discomfort."

"OK then," I said. "You and Marty run with those two aspects and I'll catch up on the file for tomorrow's motions on the Hudson case. I'm before Judge DePalma and I'd better be ready."

"And I'll get cracking on this paperwork," Sue said. "Carol deserves our best."

4 - Conversation with Harris

Harris and I had come back from our walk and settled into the lounges in my back yard, when Sarah brought us some cold drinks.

"How much longer are you going to torture your grandson?" she teased.

"Well," I replied, *"he asked the questions and I'm just filling him in on how it works in a law firm when you're buried neck-deep in a difficult case. What do you think, Harris? Want me to cut it short?"*

"Actually, Uncle Alex said he'd even excuse me from my shift flipping burgers if I was here with you figuring out a career. So, my time is your time. If I get bored, I'll tell you."

"You're in for it now, kid." Sarah's eyes twinkled. "What time are you meeting your friends tonight?"

"Not until nine-ish."

"That sounds great." Sarah was happy to have any of the grandchildren around. "I'll set up a deli spread for you when you get hungry."

Harris grinned at her. "I promise to let you know when I'm ready for lunch." Sarah walked away, and Harris turned back to face me. "So you were thinking about Aunt Mindy when you were talking to Carol?"

"Mostly," I said. *"I'd worked with a lot of women clients by then, even some who had been abused. It's tough enough for me to hear about the slapping and yelling and threatening each*

other. But having someone in front of you talking about having a husband intentionally injuring her to that extent was awful. Even seeing people shooting and maiming each other in the movies or on TV doesn't have the impact of hearing it directly from a real person. Just watching her as she told me—part hurt, part embarrassed, part pleading—pulled at my heart and made me want to help.

"That night I came home and simply held your grandma, trying to protect her from even having to listen to me recount those horrific details, yet relying on her to pull me out of that dark place."

"I guess I'll need to consider the impact of my career choice on my family, too," Harris mused. "That's a twist the school counselors haven't mentioned."

"Choosing the right life partner is more important than a career, as you'll soon see. Let's get back to the story."

5 - Strategy

Marty and I met for lunch at Manny's Cellar, a local hole-in-the-wall six steps down in the basement of the historic Fallon House on St. John Street. It was built in 1855 by one of San Jose's earliest mayors and is considered a landmark for San Jose. With smoke-stained ceilings and a rowdy bar with a blaring TV, it was largely populated by the legal community, and only a block from our office in the Community Bank Building. The waitresses were not young and pretty; they'd been around and let you know it with sarcasm and humor. As a bonus, if you wanted to know what was happening in the community or the court, you only had to sit at the bar with a beer for a half hour any day after 6 p.m. We both ordered the meatball subs with extra napkins, then got down to business.

Marty went first. "How'd DePalma treat you this morning on the Hudson case?"

"That was a motion for a vocational assessment of the wife. It should have been an easy one, but you know DePalma. He showed a lot of concern, then took everything under submission. I swear, if it weren't for the rules cutting off their paychecks if they keep cases under submission more than 60 days, we'd never hear back from him. The delay just adds another 60 days of support for wife. Hubby is pissed. But right now, I'm more concerned about the criminal aspects of the Collins case."

"You got it." Marty wiped his napkin across his mouth. "Turns out Plato Novetsky is the ADA on Collins. The charge is two counts of felony spousal battery. Robert Paladino is representing Bill. He's already been arraigned before Judge Thomas Stewart, and released on only $10,000 bail. He's back living in his house."

"Who posted it? Bondsman?"

"Nope. Daddy posted it in cash. I hear old Plato just nodded when Paladino said that it was a case for OR, but they'd agree to $10,000."

I just shook my head at the ADA's easy acceptance of Bill deserving his own recognizance in a case this brutal. "Does that mean Daddy has the juice to get the charges kicked?"

"Maybe." Marty shrugged. "But Judge Stewart has his ear to the ground and knows there would be an outcry if this just disappeared."

"I was hoping there would be a quick plea that we could take to the Family Court and ease our way with the custody and restraining order. And maybe make a personal injury case a slam dunk." I'd already contemplated Carol suing Bill for the injuries he inflicted on her. Having a conviction for a felony would make this an easy way for Carol to have some real money to get her life back on track and make a payday for the firm.

"When's the preliminary hearing?" I asked.

"Bill waived time and the prelim is set for May 7th."

"So much for a speedy trial. Damn," I said. "So, it's not likely we'll have anything useful from the criminal court until after our motions are heard?"

"Right. But we don't know that Bill's going to fight the restraining orders or temporary custody."

"If they've waived time, I bet you a beer that they will fight," I challenged.

"No way," he said. "I've bought you enough beer already. Let's get back to the office. I'll get Jules to do some more digging on Thomas Collins."

6 - Divorce Papers

March 29, 1985

At the office morning briefing, Sue told me that the preliminary papers on the Collins case would be ready for my review by noon and asked if she should set up an appointment with Carol to come in and sign.

"Sure, let's get her in ASAP," I said. "I'm sure I'll have a lot more questions for her."

"Here's one more," Marty said. "I found out that Thomas Collins is, indeed, a big shot in the development of commercial buildings. A few years back, he was one of the contractors bidding to remodel the old Sumitomo Bank building on Park Avenue when it was turned into the family courthouse. No word on why he didn't get it."

"So, maybe he does have real pull with the DA, too," I said, thinking out loud.

Marty nodded. "Looks that way. We'll know for sure in a couple of weeks. But he's clearly not a lightweight and knows his way around county politics."

The Petition was a pretty simple form. Name, rank, serial number. Check the boxes: I want my marriage dissolved. I want support, custody. I want him to pay my attorney fees. I want half the community property. I want, I want, I want.

The key to our papers was the declaration in support of the request for the restraining order. Sue had done enough of these that her efforts required very little from me other than my signature. For support, she had even prepared an approximate budget based on the expenses Carol had filled out. We estimated that Bill made $30,000 per year, but we didn't have any back-up documentation for our guess. He was required to prove his own income. Somewhere along the line we might have to do some digging about how much he is paid under the table and how much he gets from his dad, but we had enough to get things filed and the case started.

"Great job, Sue. I've signed. Let me know when Carol's scheduled."

* * * * *

Carol came in to sign the Petition the following Wednesday, April 3. She was with her friend Jill, not her mother. As she entered my office, I was blown away by the change in her. She even seemed taller now. She was still wearing the halo, but was much more relaxed. Even her hair had more sheen. She certainly wouldn't be walking in heels any time soon, but there was more confidence about her, even in the way she sat.

I asked her about the halo.

She fairly beamed. "He says I'm doing fine and the halo will likely be off at eight weeks. Mom still has to help me wash and dry, but I'm feeling much better, thank you very much!"

"That's good news," I said, wondering if the animation was because she was feeling almost human again or some fun she may have had with Jill on the way to the office. "Have you looked at the papers yet?"

We sat down side-by-side to go through the papers, while Jill left with a small wave and the assurance that she'd be in our waiting room to drive Carol home.

Carol glanced at the first page. "What is this Dissolution of Marriage stuff? Aren't I getting a divorce?"

"There is no more divorce in California, even though we still call it that," I explained. "And grounds now just require a short statement that irreconcilable differences have arisen that caused the irremediable breakdown of the marriage." I noticed Carol's confused expression. "That pretty much means you can't get along anymore. Not like in the old days when the nicest thing a couple could say in order to get a divorce was that there was extreme mental cruelty or adultery. The initial pleading we prepared in those days was at least four pages long."

I was pleased that these days we could use irreconcilable differences as the basis for dissolution, as intended by the legislature. Years ago in Santa Clara County, conservative judges wouldn't grant the dissolution if one of the parties swore they believed the marriage could be saved with some more work. The presiding judge, when accosted by the Family Law Bar, finally began assigning the cases to younger, more liberal judges, who pretty much rubber-stamped the applications.

"OK," she said. "That's definitely too much information."

She signed the Petition and went on to her Motion for Family Support and for Temporary Restraining Orders. After she read for a while, she looked up and asked, "Will he go to jail? Will I get Joey back?"

"Carol, Bill going to jail is a two-edged sword. In terms of punishment, if he pleads no contest or is found guilty of a felony, that crime is punishable by one year or more in prison, not county jail. So if he goes to prison, you will certainly get sole custody of Joey. Plus, if there is a felony on his record, we can have that admitted into evidence in all other proceedings—

including the dissolution, custody and the possible personal injury case. But it may interfere with his ability to get a job outside of Collins Construction, and then he may not have the means to pay child support." I paused, letting that scenario sink in. "However, if he gets the charges reduced to a misdemeanor...well, let's cross that bridge when we come to it. Do you have any other questions before you sign?"

"Will I have to actually speak in court?"

"Yes, you will. We will spend more time together to make sure you are ready. In the meantime, there are a few more questions I have for you."

She took a deep breath. "OK, shoot."

"First, you seem much different today without your mother. Has the tension between you let up since we talked last week?"

"Um, yes. Some. What does that have to do with anything?" She sounded defensive.

"Well, this is likely to be a long and difficult process. Your support system will play a big part in how well you hold up when things get adversarial."

"Why do you expect that?"

"Let's just say, I've been in this business almost 15 years. Your injuries are the most severe I've ever seen. They are also the most dramatic I've ever heard. My senses tell me that this will not go easily. You and I are going to have to spend some time going over your personal history, your history with Bill, your ability to lean on other people to deal with the emotional fallout in pursuing this case. You will need all the people you can find to lean on."

"I don't think my mother will be one of them."

"Has something else happened since you first came in?"

"Nothing new. I think it will be better as I get to do more for myself without her help. Dad's cool with most things, but he works a lot, too. Having to live with her while I recover and get this legal stuff taken care of ..." She trailed off, and her expression became glum. "It's just tough."

"Well," I said, trying to be comforting, "I hope you can find a way to hang in there. And you are probably going to have to live with them for a while longer." I paused for a moment, hoping she'd come up with another option. "Being with Jill seems to give you a lift," I finally ventured. "Could you live with her?"

"Jill's got her own stuff to deal with, but once in a while I can have her help out. As far as living with her and Tony...no."

"OK, it was just a thought. I want to prepare you for something else. I'm going to need to get a full history of your life with Bill before court, even before you were married. We're going to present the history of his violence toward you, how he has treated your family, and more. I just want you to be prepared and to start thinking about it. Maybe trying to put it down in writing, all in chronological order, will help you to remember and keep things straight. It will be important."

"I'll think about it...Yeah, I can start on it tomorrow."

"Good. I'll let you know when Bill is served and what the court date will be. And try to keep things with your mother on an even keel."

"I'll try. But no promises." She rose to her feet, shook my hand, and left.

* * * * *

I wanted to make sure there were no mix-ups with the papers, so I had Jules walk them through the court, then he personally served Bill at the house on Vistamont. I was able to call Carol the next day.

"Carol, we have some news. The papers have been served on Bill. Jules said Bill took them without a fuss. The next part I'm not so sure about. The hearing on support and custody is set for May 14th, which is a long way out. The good news though, is that the preliminary hearing in the Criminal Court is set for the 7th, the week prior, so we may have something to present to the judge in the dissolution."

"How will that affect me?"

"Well, if they make a deal that we can enter into evidence in the dissolution, we can probably keep you from having to testify. The criminal record should be enough."

"And if he doesn't?"

"You'll have to testify. How are you coming with the history we talked about yesterday?"

"I couldn't bring myself to start. I got the pad and pen, but it was just too painful."

"Do you have a therapist to work with?"

"No. I don't have insurance and Mom doesn't believe in them, so she won't pay."

"If you are willing, I have someone who has helped many other victims of domestic violence, and, yes, that is what you are. She can prepare you to deal with these situations."

"Will I have to pay?"

"I'm not sure. But I think you'd like working with her. In fact, with your permission, I'd like to tell her you will call her. No commitment."

"OK. What's her name?"

"Dr. Diane Gold. She's a psychologist."

* * * * *

My next call was to Diane. I had to leave a message.

"Hey, Diane, it's Steve. I think it's time I paid you that lunch I owe you. How's about lunch at Manny's Thursday? The special is French Dip. I'm heading home now; you can call me there if you can break free, or just leave a message on the office machine."

With terrible traffic, it took me about 40 minutes to get from the office to my home in Campbell—a quiet street a couple of blocks away from the Pruneyard shopping center. Converted from its original namesake fruit transportation hub, the Pruneyard was more than just a strip mall. It had a couple of high-rise office buildings, a number of restaurants, and movie theaters—more like the entire downtown of a small city. It was still 60 degrees outside at 6 p.m., so I decided to take our dog Timbur, a 65-pound Golden, for a walk before it got too much cooler or darker. Sarah asked to come along, even though with her much shorter legs she has to hustle to keep up with us both. Or that was the excuse she gave for reaching out for my free hand and holding it tight.

We walked the perimeter of the Pruneyard in just under an hour and arrived home. There was a note by the phone that one of the kids had jotted down in sloppy, teenage scrawl: Diane had called. She said she "would see you for lunch tomorrow. You're buying."

I slept much more soundly that night.

7 - Attorney Don Fraser

April 4, 1985

That morning I heard from Bill's lawyer, Donald Fraser. Great, I thought. Don had been a year behind Marty and me in law school; we'd even played pick-up basketball together at the Y. We'd never really clicked and that came out in spades during this first phone call about the case.

"Steve," he said, "I've read your papers and there is absolutely no basis for a restraining order or for Carol to have custody. Bill denies ever touching her and will explain the many ways in which she is incapable as a parent. He wants primary custody and will fight to the end to keep Joey with him."

It must have taken me a full 10 seconds of careful breathing before I could respond. "Interesting," I said. "Then how do you explain the broken neck?"

"She fell."

"Crushing two vertebrae?"

"It was an awkward fall. She's clumsy."

"My God, Don! How can you say that?" I was fairly shouting, incensed that he could even offer such a reprehensible defense.

"That's his story and I'm sure he's going to stay with it. I guess we'll see you in Court."

I probably shouldn't have slammed the phone in his ear. Attorneys can't just believe everything their clients tell them, but Carol's story made sense to me and Don's coldness made me want to scream. My experience in other cases involving spousal abuse was that while there may have been some discrepancies between stories, nobody had flat-out denied the event.

Sue dashed in from her secretarial station outside my door, her expression alarmed. Marty was two steps behind her. Apparently sounds carried in the office farther than I thought.

I told them what Don had said, then bit out, "I don't get how anybody could say that and keep a straight face!"

"Look," Marty said, his tone calming, "Bill is facing two felonies. Any kind of admission now and he'll be gone for a long, long time. So, if I were representing Bill, I'd try to come up with a story—any story—that would keep him from facing perjury charges as well as the spousal battery charges."

"But," I protested, "he's got to sign a declaration under penalty of perjury denying or otherwise explaining Carol's statement of facts!"

"And we haven't seen Bill's declaration risking that penalty of perjury yet, have we?" Marty said. "So settle down. In fact, let's go to the Y for a run at noon."

"Can't today. I'm meeting Dr. Diane for lunch. Tomorrow?"

"You're on."

8 - Psychologist Dr. Diane Gold

April 4, 1985

I was already seated at Manny's when Diane walked in. After social hugs, she pointed at my already half-empty glass of beer and raised an eyebrow.

"Lunch?"

"TGIF?" I stammered. A lame excuse, especially since it was just Thursday.

"What's really going on?" she asked, dropping in the seat across from me. Diane had a few years on me, carrying an extra 20 pounds on her short frame yet quite comfortable with it. With dirty blond hair and large, fashionably framed glasses, she made clients laugh when she referred to herself as "fluffy." She had some lingering freckles and a gap between her front teeth she didn't try to hide when she smiled—which was often.

"Rough case, rough morning," I mumbled.

"OK, tough guy, tell Dr. Diane about it." Diane had helped me with a few of my more difficult cases, holding hands, giving treatment, coaching my clients on how to pass the courtroom personality test with the judges, mostly in custody and support cases.

She ordered an iced tea and I began the story. How I met Carol, her injuries at the hands of Bill, the looming custody battle, the callous way Don Fraser was treating the matter, how I wanted to punch him.

Diane stirred her tea and held my gaze for a long moment. "You really didn't invite me out for lunch to repay a debt, did you?"

"Sorry about that, Diane. I wasn't sure where to turn and Carol seems so damned needy. I'm not even sure I'll be able to get her to give me a decent history, let alone hold together with what's coming when Don and Bill make noises that she tripped and is clumsy enough to break her own neck that way. I just want to hit them both!"

"What do you need me to do?"

"I'm not sure. You should expect a call from her soon. If she doesn't call in the next couple of days, let me know and I'll light the fire. At the very least, we need a good history of the violence, both physical and emotional. Then I'm sure she'll need some coaching on how to behave in front of a judge or jury. The jury part is in case we wind up suing Bill for the damages. And I'm thinking she could use some help on learning to cope with her mother, who is a real piece of work in her own right."

"I'll bet you want me to solve the Israeli-Palestinian mess too, right?"

I gave her my best grin. "If it's not too much trouble. Would you charge extra for that?"

"No, the Nobel Prize I'd get would be satisfaction enough." She paused. "Any idea about whether I'd be paid for all of this?"

"Only for solving the Israeli-Palestinian problem."

"Seriously, this sounds like it could be a lot of pro bono time. And I don't need any more points with the Psychological Association."

"Let me work on that. But in the meantime, would you comp us a couple of hours to assess her and get us started on the history?"

"You're still buying lunch?"

"Absolutely. And, as a bonus you and Isaac can come to dinner at our house any time."

She flashed me her wonderful smile. "Steve, I feel like the trout that just swallowed the fly, but I'll help out."

9 - Waiting

April 4-11, 1985

When I got back to the office, I found Marty in our conference room preparing for a deposition. He knew what was going on and immediately asked, "How'd it go with Diane?"

"I think she's on board. At least for a couple of hours."

"You know she'll be the key to the injury suit." It was a statement, not a question.

"Of course. You want to talk to her?"

Marty shook his head. "Not yet. Let's get the assessment and history first."

"Are we still on for a run tomorrow?" I could feel the built-up tension festering in me and needed to vent.

"Yes. Unless something else blows up."

I didn't think I could handle even one more tiny problem. My choice of profession was on the line with this case. Never before had I allowed a client's situation to impact my emotions like this, and I was worried. Had I lost my objectivity? So much for a career path as a judge, though that had never appealed to me much. What else could a washed-up attorney do?

Oh, yeah. Become a muckety-muck at one of these insane start-ups that were hiring male engineers like crazy and facing lawsuits galore from the few women who worked in those anonymous buildings under the new sexual harassment and discrimination laws. As much as their complaints may be valid, the thought of defending loutish behavior made me recoil. At least with Carol, I was comfortably on the moral side of the issue.

Timbur's tongue was hanging out by the time Sarah and I got home from our walk that night. And so was Sarah's.

* * * * *

Things were pretty calm at the office Friday morning, so Marty and I were able to get to the Y to start our run, a regular route past the San Jose Municipal Rose Gardens. Pacing ourselves side-by-side, we used this time to talk about whatever was going on, whether home, office, or global politics. Sports, the latest jokes, the courthouse gossip—nothing was off limits.

"Anything new on your rescue mission?" he asked, innocently.

"Not yet," I said. "But I'll let you know when we get the papers from Don. Thanks again for the perspective yesterday. It may take both you and Diane to keep me from going off the rails."

"You got it, partner."

I took a deep breath and shared my inner thoughts from yesterday. My professional doubts carried potential liability to the partnership, which meant that Sue's and Jules' jobs were on the line, too.

Marty scoffed. "Look, Steve, I get it. I remember when I saw my daughter all excited about going to her first prom wearing a form-fitting dress, all grown up. I'd be personalizing this case, too. But you've got to separate the good guys from the bad. There's something off about Bill, and you know it. Whether his family life was horrible or not, he's a grown man and made his choices." He added, "As did Carol. The best we can hope for is that every woman is made aware that she has options when violence starts, and acts to get out of there before an injury like that occurs. Isn't that worth fighting for?"

"Yeah, you're right. Sorry I'm being such a numbskull."

"Nothing to worry about!" Then he kicked up the pace and I couldn't talk anymore. Nice guy.

10 - Dr. Gold Talks Domestic Violence

April 12, 1985

I heard from Diane the following Friday. "What's up Dr. D?"

"I met with Carol."

"That's it?"

"On the 9th and again on the 11th."

"Any good news?"

"Maybe. There is a serious history of alcohol abuse by both Carol and Bill. He's used violence a number of times: hammerlocks, slapping. She doesn't identify it as being domestic violence because he hadn't broken any bones or sent her to the hospital before this. She seems to normalize it as part of being married, along with the abusive sex."

"Wow. I wonder where she could have gotten that idea. Maybe if that was happening between her parents. Were you able to get any kind of a date-by-date summary I can use to get her prepared for depositions? And what about her mom?"

"I'll ask about her parents. We're a bit away from the kind of chronological story line you're looking for. I'll need to see her at least twice more to have anything resembling useful information. She's really skittish about her mom. I just wanted to let you know that there is a lot going on here and she really needs treatment. From my perspective, it is a classic DV case that left her with PTSD."

I knew that DV stood for domestic violence and that Post-Traumatic Stress Disorder had become accepted as an official disorder from the Diagnostic and Statistical Manual II—the bible in the psycho-therapeutic community. "Any chance there's medical insurance to cover you for this?"

"Nope. And there's a limit to my pro bono time. I'm going to have to start billing someone, soon."

"Will she go to her mom for help? Maybe with a note from you?"

"That's going to be a prime subject for our next meeting. I'm set to see her again on the 16th and I'm going to bring it up. And, FYI, I'm not confident that she's ready to take care of Joey. Despite outward appearances, she's barely functional herself."

"You mean that Bill's parents could wind up raising this kid by default?" When Marty had raised that specter yesterday, I hadn't really considered this possibility for their next generation.

"If Carol's parents won't take more responsibility, that's the most likely case," Diane said.

"Well, if you can get Carol to bring her parents in, they might step up to protect her and Joey."

Diane's resigned sigh carried clearly through the telephone and into my ear. "That's a conversation you might need to have with them. At this point I have a waiver that lets me talk to you as her attorney, but that's it."

"Good work. Keep me in the loop."

"Will do. Talk to you next week. Bye."

11 - Bill Collins' Declaration

April 12, 1985

Sue walked in with the morning mail. On top was a response from Don to our Motions, plus a package of requests for information Don wanted from Carol. There was also a notice to take her deposition on May 1, six days before the preliminary hearing and thirteen days before our hearing.

His reply to our declaration was that it was all false. Bill's declaration swore she made stuff up all the time to make him look bad. I stormed into Marty's office with the news. He talked me down off the ceiling and said he'd have probably done something similar in the same circumstances.

"Understanding and agreeing are not the same thing," I replied. "But thanks, anyway."

Returning to my office, I took a deep breath and placed a call to Don. I had to leave a message and it was 3 p.m. before he got back to me.

"Hey, Don. I got your package. Nice."

"I thought you'd like it." I could almost hear his grin through the phone line.

"I don't think we'll be ready for depositions that soon. Carol is still pretty raw and sorting out what happened to her."

"She seemed pretty clear in her declaration. I'm entitled to ask her about that before we go to court."

"You going to force me to seek a protective order?"

"Do what you have to do. I expect her in my office on time, like it says on the notice."

"So much for cooperation. Could we maybe agree to some temporary orders keeping them apart, set up a little visitation with Joey, and maybe some support? We could continue the hearing and reschedule the deposition."

"Nope," was his terse reply. "Bill doesn't want his chances for another job to be lost due to another restraining order."

"I suppose we can just ask the judge at the prelim. He has the authority and the DA should have enough evidence for it."

"If you think so, go for it. My walking papers are to make you work for everything. I'll deny that I said that, but don't go looking for any cooperation."

"I hear you." And slammed the phone down so he could hear me, too.

I poked my head out of the office to see who was still around. Sue was at her desk with a form in the typewriter and something blinking on the screen of the word processor. I didn't want to risk making her lose her chain of thought, so I looked through the glass panel next to the door of Marty's office. He was behind his desk, chatting with Jules, who had taken one of the client chairs across from him.

Marty waved me in.

"Looks like a conspiracy in progress to me," I said, trying to be light, pointing at the two of them.

"From the look on your face, you're the one needing aid and comfort again," Marty said, obviously not buying my act. "Grab a seat. We were just going over the calculations on the speed the defendant was travelling before he hit Mrs. Williams in her Mercedes. Remember?"

"Isn't she the one who just had the tri-level fusion in her lumbar spine?"

"Yup. That was six weeks ago and she's not recovering well."

"What's the plan?"

"If she doesn't turn a corner soon, we may have to get a second opinion on the rehab. I really don't want to do that. Dr. Anderson has been spot-on for us so far, and I don't want to get him pissed at us."

"You got that right! Hey, Jules, any more information on the Bill Collins prelim?"

Jules shook his head. "My guy at the DA's says they've been getting pressure to have it reduced to a misdemeanor. Then they may take a nolo contendere plea."

I slumped in my chair, disheartened that Bill might avoid this trial by simply not contesting misdemeanor charges. How could we ever end this kind of influence?

Marty piped in. "Ouch. Nolo to the misdemeanor means we wouldn't be able to use the plea in the divorce or a personal injury case. Whose butt do we have to kiss to make that not happen?"

"We're not there yet," Jules replied. "I hear that the ADA, Plato, has the surgeon ..." Jules consulted his notes, "a Dr. Angelo Anton subpoenaed for the prelim. I think we ought to be there for that. It might even get you a free conversation with the good doctor."

"Have either of you heard of Anton?" I asked. They both shook their heads.

"I'll be talking to Dr. Anderson about Williams again on Monday." Marty scratched his jaw. "I'll make a note to ask him about Anton."

Thinking out loud, I said, "That'll be the 15th. It will give us a chance to get to the Doc before the prelim and maybe find out a little more."

"Let's hope so." Marty's lack of enthusiasm was telling of our slim odds of success.

12 - Something Positive

April 16, 1985

The Tuesday morning mail cheered me up. Sue came in, holding up the Order on the Hudson Motion.

"Judge DePalma ruled already," she said, thrusting the papers at me.

"Wow," I said. "Only about 50 days earlier than I'd expected. Let's see."

The Order granted our request for a vocational assessment. But the real surprise was that we were awarded attorney fees. Judge DePalma even blasted the wife's attorney for making us bring the motion in the first place. This meant that Mrs. Hudson would have to see our vocational counselor who would assess her employability and the range of earnings she might expect, a critical element in the computation of spousal support.

Mostly, it gave me hope that he'd help out on the Collins fee application, as well as recognizing Carol would need more professional help from Dr. D both now and probably in the future. If not, I feared Carol would become another lost soul, abandoned by the legal process.

* * * * *

Harris stopped me. "It sounds like good news is pretty rare. I'm not sure I'd want to be in a job where it's mostly bad news."

"Actually," I replied, "we usually have much more good news than bad. It's just that sometimes, in a particular case, it seems like you're always rowing against the tide."

"And waiting for-ev-er," he said, drawing the word out in that annoying teenage mannerism. "Why does it take so long to make a decision, anyway?"

"I wish I could tell you," I chuckled. "Hours, days, and weeks have been wasted waiting for a judge to make up his mind. But in fairness, I guess they have a lot of cases to consider, and lots of time spent in the courtroom, too. Plus, with the addition of PCs to our lives, it seems that the legal profession made it their duty to churn out more reams of documents than before, when fixing typos meant starting from scratch. The judge has to read them all sometime."

Harris sighed. "I guess. But I can't believe being a lawyer means all this waiting for every case! Didn't you just want to do something to help Carol more?"

"Remember, you asked me to tell you about a memorable case, not a typical one, and that is what we're talking about. For some reason, I always seem to learn more from cases and situations that make me respond to adversity. Any lawyer that tells you he wins every time is either lying or will only take cases that seem like easy victories. The practice of law is about helping people in difficult situations. Most times, that translates to discomfort for the lawyer as well."

"Makes sense," he said.

13 - The State Fund for Victims

April 16, 1985

Sue walked into my office with a troubled expression, never a good sign. "I've outlined a request for a Protective Order for Carol regarding the depositions set for May 1st," she said, "but I'm getting pushback from her on the documents and the rest of the discovery we're supposed to have for Don by May 13th. Can you do something about it?"

"You've talked with her?"

"Yes. Carol has made a lot of promises but hasn't come up with anything useful. Have you spoken to Dr. Gold lately?"

"I guess I'd better go out on a limb and call her."

Picking up the phone, I immediately called Diane, but had to leave a message asking her to call me back, then remembered she was supposed to see Carol the next day sometime. I didn't hear back from Diane until Wednesday.

"Steve," she said, "we aren't going to be able to push this one too hard. What I've got now is that Bill did a real job in making sure she was estranged from her family. That's what allowed him to escalate against her—he'd cut her off from her support system and she can't figure out how to rebuild it. This Jill is the only person left for her."

"Will she be able to help us meet our discovery deadlines?"

"Probably not. And, at this point, I'm not sure how she'll stand up to even the mildest cross-examination at the hearing."

"We've got almost four weeks until then. You have any magic left?" Dr. D has pulled witnesses together for me in a lot of cases. Yet this was as negative as I'd ever heard her.

"I'll see her again Thursday. Then it's going to be waiting for our friend Mr. Green. I warned you I could only do so much pro bono work until Mr. Green shows me the money."

"So, she's not ready to ask mommy and daddy for financial help?"

"From what I've gleaned, that request would be denied. And it would cost her too much emotionally to even ask."

"Looks like I'll be at risk too, if the judge doesn't award us fees and a budget for medical."

About a half hour later, Marty knocked on my door, opened it without waiting for an answer and walked in with a grin on his face.

"Good news," Marty said. "Doc Anderson says your man Anton is a good one."

"What does that mean?"

"First, he doesn't hate lawyers. Second, he knows what he's doing with a scalpel. Third, he knows what he's doing on the stand. He'll help the DA get Bill bound over for trial."

"Then I'd better get ahold of him. Any news about a plea?"

Marty shrugged. "Nope. But I think you and I need to take a field trip to criminal court for the prelim."

"You want to come with us?"

"I'm free that morning but have to prepare for depositions the next day. I'd like to see the Doc in action as much as you would. It would be good to have another surgeon in our positive data bank."

"OK. I'll have Sue make sure it's on Carol's calendar and call Doctor Anton's office to see if we can set up a telephone conversation before then."

14 - Protective Order Required

I called Dr. Gold first thing Friday morning. I had to leave a message again; happily, she called back within the hour.

"A little anxious, are we?" I recognized her tongue-in-cheek humor.

"More than a little. If we are going to reply to discovery or apply for a protective order, I need to know soon."

"Well, I have a partial answer for you. She has suppressed a lot of the violence but is opening up to me. It's clear that Carol has post-traumatic stress from the abuse she's suffered. Her well-being has been dependent upon Bill's moods and the vibes she gets from him. She has been doing this for so long now that her world has narrowed to whatever Bill has allowed. She has been looking to him to decide whether she has value in any situation. When he is nice to her following an eruption, this gives her value. Humanity. She doesn't yet have it within herself to repair this sense of self. It's something I'll have to work on with her." She paused.

"And this means …?"

"She will still be too fragile to endure a deposition for a while. I think you'd better apply for the protective order. I'll have a declaration to that effect for you by this afternoon."

"I always feel more secure when I know where I'm going."

"Don't we all," she replied, adding, "Mr. Green didn't show up, but we may have a way."

"What's that?"

"There is a state fund for victims of domestic violence that pays for housing and treatment. I'm not sure what the cap is, but it looks like my time won't be a total write-off."

"Does that mean you'll continue to help?"

"Let me follow up with the fund. But yeah, I will for a while."

"Dr. D, you're the best!" I said it with my best Andy Rooney voice.

"Don't I know it. And don't you ever forget it."

"I won't. Cross my heart. But seriously, are you getting any feel for the duration and magnitude of violence she's suffered?"

"You know the cycle, Steve." Diane's tones carried a mixture of resignation and compassion. "A minor blip, some cooling, a bigger blip, some more cooling, etcetera, etcetera. Then comes the first slap or physical confrontation. Depending on how big it is, they'll go into apology and courting. Then things ramp up again. These two have been through it many times, starting before they were married."

"Any other significant physical altercations?"

"Well, she says that he once slammed the door of his car on her hand when she looked in to see what he was doing. Oh, and he threw a full can of beer at her when she'd asked him if he hadn't already had enough to drink." She exhaled in a long, drawn-out sigh. "Their sex life was a mess. She didn't even comprehend that her duty as a wife didn't mean he could rape her whenever he felt like it. The way she describes it, his idea of foreplay was to tell her to brace herself." She paused, and I could just picture her running her fingers through her hair in frustration. She continued, "If she was wearing a nightgown, he'd rip it off. If he was feeling considerate, he'd bring some lube to bed, but that was the exception. She couldn't begin to count the number of times this went on."

"So why didn't she get out?" I asked.

"By the time the serious violence started, he'd already isolated her from her family and friends. According to her, her dad was still mildly supportive, but her mom was against the marriage in the first place and never missed a chance to tell her so."

"Was there any violence between her parents?"

"I don't think so," she said. "At least nothing physical. Maybe some emotional stuff—by her mom."

"Tough luck all around," I murmured, thankful for my close circle of family and friends.

"And then there is the baby, the lack of finances, her total dependence on him," Diane added. "Just another classic case."

We were quiet for a moment. Finally I said, "I've read that spousal rape is more prevalent than we'd like to think. But we don't see a lot of broken necks."

"Spend a Saturday night at the E.R.," she chided. "You'd be surprised at the level of violence based on the injuries that come in."

"I'll take your word for it. And I'll start the application for a Protective Order to get her deposition put on hold. Thanks again, Diane."

I had another thought. "When are you seeing Carol again?"

"Let me check. I see we've got her coming in on Monday, the 22nd at 2 o'clock and again next Thursday, the 25th at 11. So I may have a timeline and clearer picture for you by next Friday."

"Well, I'll have to get the Protective Order to the Motion Judge by Tuesday morning on the 23rd. Give me a call next week when you have more."

"Will do." With that, she hung up.

I called Sue in and sketched out the Protective Order requirements to get her started. "I've got to give Don at least 12 hours notice of the application. Do we know who is on the motion calendar next week?"

"Your best friend, DePalma. He's your all-purpose judge on the case."

"Well, we could do worse."

"This is going to be ex parte, right? Carol asked me if she would have to attend."

"Please call her back and tell her no, and explain the lawyers will meet with Judge DePalma in his chambers office without the clients."

"She'll sure be relieved," Sue commented.

"I want to be able to fax everything to DePalma on Monday, as early as possible. Can you do that?"

"I'll do my best, boss. It's already Friday afternoon, and I was about to leave for the weekend. But, duty calls!" Sue hustled out of my office, and I was sure she would meet the deadline, as usual.

15 - Neurosurgeon Dr. Angelo Anton

April 19, 1985

Marty was in his office. He said that it looked like everything was in place for the prelim. A few minutes later, Sue poked her head and announced my callback from Dr. Anton, so I hustled to my desk.

After the introductions, I got right to it. "Doctor, I'm representing Carol Collins in her divorce. Dr. Diane Gold, a psychologist, is working with Carol to get her to a stage where she can testify and participate on her own behalf in this case."

"No." He stopped me there. "I don't want to be involved in her divorce. I have nothing to offer."

I had expected this response. "Actually, you do," I said. "Part of this is an application for a restraining order against her husband, Bill Collins. A crucial part of that is the proof that the mechanics of her broken neck are not consistent with Bill's story."

"What's his story?"

"That she fell, is what his lawyer told me."

"What a load of crap that is!" His voice resonated with disgust. "The injury is totally consistent with her story of being in a full-Nelson headlock. I've seen some injuries that were similar, usually in wrestlers, but none as severe as this one."

"If you'll just say that, it would make a big difference. The husband and lawyer are planning to make this as difficult as possible for Carol and we need all the help we can get."

"I can see that now." Anton sounded really concerned. "Get Carol to sign a written consent to have me release my records. I'll have my secretary send you copies and a cover letter explaining how my findings are consistent with her description of the attack."

"Thank you, Doctor. By the way, are you going to be at the preliminary hearing on the 7th?"

"Yes, I've been subpoenaed."

"I'm planning to be there with Carol. I'd like to meet you there."

"Good. I'll see you then."

I went back to Marty's office and gave him the positive news about Doctors Anton and Gold.

"I'm happy for you," he said, nodding his head for emphasis. "Hopefully, some good stuff will finally happen on this one."

"Thanks," I said. "Do you and Beth want to catch dinner and a movie Saturday?"

"Works for me. I have no Idea what Beth has planned. But if we're going to get together, I'll bet our ladies already have it worked out."

That Saturday, we saw *Back to the Future* and had a nice dinner. An old-fashioned double date. Music we could relate to: I always loved "Johnny B. Goode."

16 - Motions & Protective Orders

April 22-23, 1985

By late Monday morning I'd signed off on the application for the Protective Order and had it faxed to the court and to Don Fraser. We were supposed to appear before DePalma the next morning at 8:30.

I was feeling pretty good, so Marty and I walked the four blocks to Original Joe's for lunch. Their burgers on French bread were legendary. You could sit at a counter and watch the chefs at work or find a booth with wood paneling. The waiters all wore tuxedos; If they didn't have grey hair, they had none at all. We kept the conversation light and only around social matters and sports, no work issues allowed.

When we got back to the office. Sue gave me a message from Don Fraser with her usual dry insight into Don's state of mind based on his tone of voice on phone. "Let's just say he wasn't happy about having to respond to the ex parte motion."

I placed a call to Don and braced myself.

"Steve, what do you think you are going to accomplish with this?" Don challenged. "If we can't take her deposition, I'll object to her giving testimony in court two weeks later!"

"Calm down, Don. I'll let you take her deposition as soon as Dr. Gold says she's ready, and not a day sooner. Can we stipulate that I can take Bill's deposition the same day?"

"I'm thinking Carol's deposition may take two days, but you can take Bill's when we finish with her. If there is still a case."

"Then I guess I'll have to ask the court to allow sessions of no more than two hours on any day with Carol. I'll abide the same for Bill."

"You can't start with Bill until I'm completely finished with Carol."

"Sounds like something else we'll have to lay on DePalma. Unless you'd stipulate to a discovery master?"

"Only if DePalma orders it."

"See you tomorrow morning."

* * * * *

At 8:30 Tuesday morning, Don and I were both waiting outside the door to Judge DePalma's chambers. His bailiff let us in. The judge was at his desk, his back to the window, in shirtsleeves. There was a conference table extending from the front of his desk creating a T-shape with three chairs on each side. Don and I went to opposite sides of the conference table. I opened my mouth to start but the judge held up his hand.

"Mr. Fraser," he began, "can you tell me in 10 words or less why I should deny the request to postpone Mrs. Collins' deposition until she is better able to participate?"

After a beat, Don replied, "It would prejudice our ability to cross-examine her at the hearing. Sorry, Your Honor, that was 11 words."

"Is Mr. Collins denying that he broke her neck?"

"Yes, Your Honor. He claims she tripped and fell. That she is clumsy and falsely accuses him of many things."

The judge looked at me with a raised eyebrow. "Mr. Gregory," he said, then waited.

"Your Honor, we have a declaration from the neurosurgeon, Dr. Anton, that the injuries could not have happened in a trip and fall; they are consistent with Mrs. Collins' description of the events."

"Hmm." Judge DePalma considered the arguments for a long moment. "I'm inclined to grant the Protective Order based on those representations. If they prove false, I'll reverse the order and impose sanctions. So, no depositions until she's been cleared by the psychologist. Anything else gentlemen?"

"Yes," I said. "Mr. Fraser has informed me that he wants to depose Mrs. Collins over two days. I have suggested that she is likely to be ready for a two-hour session long before she could stand up to the schedule Mr. Fraser seeks. Also, I'd like to be able to begin Mr. Collins' deposition, something Mr. Fraser opposes until he's completely finished with Mrs. Collins."

"What's going on Mr. Fraser? This doesn't seem like your usual style."

"My client believes he's being defamed by these accusations. He doesn't want to make it any easier on her to continue to do so."

"Refreshingly honest, Mr. Fraser," the judge acknowledged with a wry expression. "I fully understand, and will be prepared to grant appropriate sanctions if this behavior continues. Do you understand?"

"Yes, Your Honor," Don replied, well chastised.

"Do you need a discovery master?"

I looked at Don, then back to the judge. "Your Honor, I will make an application if we run into further problems."

I'd included a proposed order with the application. Judge DePalma signed it and handed it to me. "Then that will be all, gentlemen." Don and I exited the chambers.

Once out in the hall, I turned to face Don. "I don't know whether to thank you or curse you."

"Don't worry about it," he said with a smile. "Now I can go back to my guy and tell him, legitimately, that he is going to lose big time if we continue with his strategy. Do you have a copy of the doc's declaration for me?"

"I should get it by the end of today. Tomorrow, at the latest. I'll have responses to your Request for Production of Documents in a few days. How are you coming with our discovery?"

"He hasn't provided us with anything. I doubt that he will until after the arraignment. Let's talk then."

* * * * *

Harris jumped in again. "So the judge believed you? Does that mean you won?"

"Yes and no," I said. "What we learned was that Don had been following instructions from Bill or Bill's dad. Both personally and professionally, I think that just doing whatever your client wants is not the best way to represent the client's actual interests. But by now, I understood what Don was doing: keeping us away until something was resolved in the criminal case. If Don had been honest with me, we could have saved a lot of attorneys' fees and aggravation. All I can really say is that I knew Don was getting paid to throw up roadblocks. And there was no way to know what he was really thinking.

"Since then, a number of cases have come out of the appellate courts that approve of fining lawyers for doing what Don was doing. But in the 80s, many lawyers considered being an obstructionist was simply part of vigorous advocacy."

"Just like TV," Harris commented.

17 - Valuing Medical Professionals

April 23, 1985

Later that afternoon I heard from Dr. Gold. "We had a great session today," she began.

"What do you mean? Did you get paid?"

"Not *that* great," she chuckled. "But the state fund should help, up to $7,500. Carol is starting to trust me and the process. I think we'll have something substantive for you after our next session. Gotta run. My next patient is waiting."

"Thanks, talk with you later."

As soon as I'd hung up the phone, Sue came in with the package from Dr. Anton. It was exactly as promised. I had her fax a copy of the letter to Don, then went to see Marty with the medical records. He took two minutes studying them, then looked at me, his expression grim.

"She really was close to being a quad," Marty said. "The crushing was the cervical 2–3 inter-space with a partial tear of the dorsal cervical ligaments. All consistent with Carol's description of what had happened to her. This doc knows what he's doing and how to say it. His report shows that he's going to be a great witness. Are we going ahead with the injury case?"

"I hope so, partner. I don't know if Bill has the ability to pay damages, so I won't be able to assess it until we get the discovery."

"Too bad. This should be worth a mid-six figure settlement, easy. Our fee on a half-million dollars would give us a nice cushion."

"Yeah, and you'd get to try the case," I said, trying to show excitement. Marty was way better than me with juries, always eager to strut his stuff. For me, the fact that Carol had to suffer irreparably in order for us to earn our keep as attorneys and stay in business to help the next victim stayed front and center. She didn't deserve this. "But right now, I don't know if he's worth one dollar or a million dollars, so we're just speculating. But if we hit it, this is the kind of case that should get punitive damages."

"Don't I know it!" Marty said, dreamily.

18 - The Court Calendar

April 26, 1985

That Friday, we sent Don our replies to his discovery requests even though it was 10 days early. We didn't have much to say because all the records were in Bill's possession, and that we would respond with more when we learned more. But we did reference the records from Dr. Anton and noted that there was a long history of violence directed at Carol by Bill. We said that details were emerging and that we would provide a more comprehensive report when additional information became available.

Then we sat back to wait. Bill had another week to respond to our motion. Our all-too-frequent experience was that only on the last day would the opposing attorney beg for an extension to complete their production of documents or interrogatories. Then, they would give us papers and answers to the written questions that were deficient. We fully expected this case would result in requiring us to formally ask the judge to force them to properly respond. Worst case, it might take three or four months to actually get anything useful.

* * * * *

"Why do you always talk about dates and times?" Harris asked.

"When you watch a program on TV or a movie, they move from scene to scene in what seems like a day or two. In real life,

divorce cases usually play out over six months to two years, depending on the degree of cooperation. And personal injury cases frequently take four to five years. A lawyer's life is controlled by the courts' calendar and timelines with deadlines. In many ways, managing the calendar can be the toughest part of practice. But, in a way, think about your school year: you know when your finals are going to be, when your papers are due, and when your mid-terms will be. To do well, you have to pace your work so it isn't all done the night before when you can miss an assignment."

"Cool analogy," he said, nodding his head. "Yeah, I hate all-nighters. I always seem to miss something."

19 - Checking in with Dr. Gold & Carol

May 3, 1985

I busied myself with my other cases for seven days until the following Friday. The preliminary hearing was the next Tuesday, and I needed to check in with everybody involved. Sue confirmed Dr. Anton was going to be at the hearing, while I called Dr. Gold.

"Diane," I asked, "how's she doing?"

"How's who doing?"

"Sorry, we've got so many cases together right now. Oh, wait! No, we don't."

"OK, wise guy. I guess I deserved that. Carol is continuing to fill in details. She knows she will have to be there for the prelim and is scared silly about having to face Bill in court."

"Do you know if the DA has talked with her yet?"

"She hasn't said anything about that in our sessions."

"OK. I'll give her a call and get her ready."

"Should I be at the prelim?" Diane asked.

"I don't think there should be a need. It's unlikely she'll have to take the stand with the neurosurgeon there." I paused. "On second thought, you may find it interesting, and you could probably attest to her inability to testify if things get rough. How does your Tuesday morning look?"

"I'll double-check my schedule," she said, laughing.

I took a minute to gather my thoughts before placing my next call to Carol. We hadn't talked directly for a while.

"Carol," I began, "I wanted to talk with you before the preliminary hearing scheduled for next Tuesday. Have you heard from the DA?"

"Somebody from their office called to remind me about the hearing. I'm scheduled to meet with someone from there on Monday at 10:30."

"Would you like to do the preparation at my office?"

"The investigator said she'd come to my house. I'm still staying with my mom."

"We could still do it at my office if you prefer. Would your mom being present be a problem for you?"

"Dr. Diane has been a big help, but me and Mom, um, we still aren't exactly best friends, if you know what I mean."

"Got it. How are you planning to get to Tuesday's hearing?"

"Their investigator offered to pick me up." She sounded relieved.

"OK. So, do you want to do the prep at your folks' house or my office?"

"The house. Getting downtown is still a big deal for me."

"Are you OK if I come and sit in?"

We went over a few details and agreed I'd be at her parents' house a half hour before the investigator got there. She promised to let me know if there were any changes.

20 - Meeting at Carol's Parents' House

May 6, 1985

I was at the house at 10 a.m., and pulled into the circular driveway. I'd expected something nice and wasn't disappointed. Almaden is an upper-middle-class neighborhood in southwest San Jose. The Polansky house, surrounded by oak trees, adorned the crest of a hill overlooking the exclusive Almaden Country Club. One of the double doors at the entry opened as I approached. Carol was standing there wearing a soft medical collar, a bright yellow sweatshirt and tight blue jeans.

"Look at you," she said. "Right on time."

I smiled. She waved her arm as my signal to enter, and I was stunned by the immediate visual impact of the facing glass wall inviting me to view the lush green fairways of the golf course and the sprawling valley beyond. Carol led me to the left into a family room with couches, a TV and a carpet littered with toys.

Carol's mom Arlene sat on one of the couches. Her dad was at work, Carol explained. A young boy I presumed to be Joey ignored our entrance, too busy playing with some blocks at our feet. I watched him for a couple of beats, then turned to Carol with my eyebrows raised.

"Mary, Bill's mom, dropped him off last night," she said with a shrug. "I think she wants him here so that she and his dad can be at Bill's side at the hearing tomorrow, and someone from my family won't be able to attend."

"How's he doing?" I paused. "Was he happy to see you?"

She shrugged. "Joey is Joey. I think he was happy to see me. I sure was happy to see him again. It's been over two months now."

"I hadn't realized you'd been kept away from him that long." I tried to convey compassion for her dilemma, and held back my cynicism.

Her eyes welled up with tears. "I still can't lift him up or really play with him and he doesn't understand."

"Look at it this way: you're making progress," I encouraged. "You have Joey here. You're wearing a soft collar instead of a halo. When did the halo come off?"

"A couple of weeks ago!" She smiled. "Now it is all about physical therapy for probably another month, maybe more. I wear the soft collar more as a safety reminder and take it off when I can relax."

"How's the eating going?"

She frowned. "Well, this sweatshirt is about the only top I have that doesn't have food stains on it. But I don't need anybody to feed me any more, so that's all good."

"That's great to hear. By the way, I spoke to Dr. Anton about a week ago," I said. "He's going to be at court tomorrow, so maybe he'll give us a sneak preview then. But the reason I wanted to be here early was to talk to you a little about what's likely to happen tomorrow."

I was about to launch into my explanation of what would happen at the prelim, when the doorbell rang. Carol left to answer the door and returned with the DA's investigator, similar to Carol in age and build. She introduced herself as Rosa Hernandez with an infectious smile and easy-going, confident demeanor, great for putting a witness at ease. Arlene stayed with Joey in the family room while the three of us adjourned to the living room. Carol sat down gingerly.

"Please just call me Rosa," the investigator began, flashing that great smile. "I'm going to try to explain what is going to happen tomorrow. The preliminary hearing is just for a judge to decide whether there is enough evidence to proceed to a trial on the crimes charged. The defendant, your ex, does not have to present any evidence; it is up to the district attorney to put on evidence and for the judge to decide if there is enough for a reasonable jury to find that the defendant has committed the crimes charged. We do this in California when a defendant has been charged with a felony—a crime punishable by a year or more in prison. Any questions so far?"

"Will I have to testify?" Carol immediately asked, her voice carrying a familiar whiff of panic.

"Probably. That's why I'm here: to get you ready."

Rosa asked Carol to recount the events of the night of February 9th. Carol seemed to wilt as she talked. It was like pulling teeth to get Carol to look up and speak above a whisper as she relived the attack, moment by moment. She picked at her fingernails. I was impressed with how well Rosa managed Carol's anxiety.

Rosa paused and flipped through her papers.

"Will I have to talk about the other times?" Carol muttered.

Rosa looked up from her notes. "Other times?"

"Yes, the other times Bill raped me and beat me."

Rosa appeared stunned. "I didn't realize there were other times. There was nothing in your file."

Carol raised her head and met Rosa's gaze. "Nobody asked. I don't want him to get off because the judge might think this was a one-time thing," she said with certainty.

Finally! Carol showed some steel, I thought, and jumped in. "I understand Dr. Anton will be there tomorrow as well. Have you or Plato Novetsky been in touch with him?"

Rosa shook her head. "Sounds like you know more about this than I do. I'll be checking in with Mr. Novetsky, as the ADA on this case, right after lunch and make sure we're ready. I'll also tell him that there are multiple other charges we can add. If I get the OK from him, I'll spend some more time with Carol on the details." She turned to Carol. "Will you still need a ride to court?"

"No, thank you," Carol replied. "I'll be riding with my dad. He's taking the day off work and wants to bring me. My mom will stay here with Joey."

Rosa informed Carol that the hearing would be in the new Hall of Justice on Hedding Street, not the Market Street courthouse or Park Avenue.

I was worried that Carol wouldn't be as at ease in this venue. The new HOJ was much more utilitarian than Market Street or Park. The courtrooms for preliminary hearings were almost factory-like, with tables full of files in boxes, many ADAs and paralegals milling around. There were usually five to ten public defenders and private attorneys sitting in the auditorium seats, waiting for their clients' cases to be filed or talking with the ADAs assigned to the cases. Defendants out on bail would be sitting with their attorneys. No juries are at arraignments and the area that would normally house the juries are filled with defendants. There are usually a few extra armed deputies on standby in the courtroom, hoping they won't be needed.

However, Rosa didn't disclose any of those details and took her leave. I hastily told Carol she had done great, I'd see her tomorrow, and followed Rosa out the front door.

"Wait up a second," I called out. She stopped next to her car. "Has Plato been under any pressure on this one?" I asked.

She looked at me quizzically. "What do you mean?"

"Do you know if anybody is pushing him to reduce the charges or accept a minimum plea?"

"Not that I'm aware of, and with the new information about multiple prior rapes, I'll push hard, instead, for adding additional felony counts."

"Thanks. That's what I wanted to hear. See you tomorrow."

21 - The Preliminary Hearing

May 7, 1985

The hearing was scheduled for 10 a.m.; I arrived at 9:30, along with Marty and Jules, both of whom wanted to see what was going to happen. Sue was left minding the office.

Rosa had saved seats for Carol and her father, Arnold, whom I'd never met. He was taller than I'd expected for some reason, probably six feet, a little heavy, straight-backed, black hair, and sported a five-o'clock shadow first thing in the morning. He had a firm handshake and quite a protective attitude toward Carol. Overall, he seemed a whole lot warmer than Arlene, with a wide, easy smile, and dark eyes that had the kind of wrinkles at the edges suggesting he was usually quick to laugh.

I glanced around to make sure Dr. Anton had arrived. He sat in the back row by himself, perusing a thick file. Reassured, I turned my attention to the principals of today's hearing seated at the front.

It was the first time I'd seen Bill, who was wearing a navy blazer, tan slacks, a light blue button-down shirt and a paisley tie covering his imposing build. Tall, maybe 200 pounds, he looked like someone who lifted weights. His neatly trimmed, stubby beard covered some obvious acne scars, and his short brown hair framed a kind of flat face with a serious expression; at least he wasn't playing around with the situation.

Bill was flanked by a couple I took to be Bill's parents. Even sitting down, his father looked taller than Bill, with a razor-cut full head of the same light-brown hair and wearing a tan suit. His mother looked like an aging cheerleader, sporting a similar blue blazer and charcoal slacks. I guessed that stylish cordovan penny loafers adorned her feet.

Promptly at 10 a.m. the bailiff told us to rise. "Court is now in session," he announced. "The Honorable Thomas Stewart, presiding."

"This is People versus Collins," the court clerk said, and recited the case number.

The judge asked counsel to state their appearances.

Plato stood and said, "Plato Novetsky for the People, Your Honor." He sat back down.

Bill's lawyer stood and announced, "Robert Paladino for the defendant, William Collins."

Plato and Robert were a contrast in appearances. Plato was wearing a brown suit that seemed to be made of separates from Macy's, permanently wrinkled, while Robert was wearing a charcoal pin-striped Armani suit. He looked athletic and in control. He had a shaved head and rimless glasses. Plato wore thick tortoise shell glasses and his tousled hair fell well beyond his collar.

Robert raised his index finger. "If it may please the court, we have a stipulation."

I caught Marty's eye, shocked at the role reversal. Usually the DA asked for a stipulation, never the defense counsel. What was going on?

Even the judge seemed surprised. He looked at the ADA. "Is that right Mr. Novetsky?"

Plato rose to his feet again. "It is, Your Honor. We understand that, while the defendant has pled not guilty, he is going to waive the preliminary hearing."

"Really?" The judge looked to the other table. "Mr. Paladino?"

"Correct, Your Honor. We recognize that, while we deny the charges, the State has enough evidence to pass the minimum bar of a preliminary hearing."

"Very well then. The defendant will stand trial on the charges as read. Shall we discuss a trial date?"

"Not yet, Your Honor." Plato took the lead again. "We are considering additional charges and we understand that the victim may not be sufficiently able to testify for a while. Since the defendant has waived his right to a speedy trial, we thought we could return in three months and revisit the trial date. And the restraining order will remain in effect."

"You don't want me to set the trial now, then apply for a continuance, if necessary?" The judge was obviously uneasy with the process Plato had proposed, a far departure from the usual insistence on a hearing, then a quick trial date.

"No, Your Honor," said Plato. "There are a lot of things we're talking about."

Marty nudged my elbow and shot me a knowing look. That usually meant some kind of plea deal.

"Very well counsel," the judge said. "So ordered. The restraining order will remain in effect for one year. Next case." The gavel came down and the audience started buzzing. I tried to grab Plato, but he avoided me and ducked out a side door.

I found Rosa, "What just happened? Did you talk to Plato yesterday after our session with Carol?"

Rosa looked like she'd had the wind knocked out of her. Marty, Jules, Arnold, Carol, and even Dr. Anton gathered around us.

"Mr. Novetsky and I talked yesterday," Rosa said. "I gave him my assessment of Carol's ability to testify, checked in about Dr. Anton, and Mr. Novetsky never said a word when I told him about the history of prior rapes and batteries. I've never seen a defense attorney pass up a chance to rattle a prosecution witness and maybe get the charges dropped."

"This smells like the fix is in." I looked at Jules, who only shrugged.

Rosa shook her head. "I don't think that's possible. This office has always gone after rapists. Hard."

"I'm glad I didn't have to testify today," Carol said. "But what just happened?"

Rosa turned toward Carol and placed a hand on Carol's arm. "This was unusual. Remember that I told you today was about having enough evidence for the criminal case to continue?"

Carol nodded.

"Bill's attorney said that there was enough evidence so there would be no point to putting witnesses on the stand," Rosa explained. "Usually, defense attorneys want to hear what the witnesses will say to prepare for a cross-examination at trial, later. Given the agreements they made with the judge, we don't know when the trial will be, but I will check in with Mr. Novetsky and see whether we're going to file additional charges, or what's going to happen."

"I think I've got it figured out," Marty said, a knowing smile on his face. "If there is no publicity about the evidence produced at a prelim, the press has nothing to chew on. And when we go to take Bill's deposition, or do other discovery, he can be evasive and take the Fifth."

I turned to explain to Carol. "That means—"

"I know what that means," Carol cut me off. "He won't have to say anything that could be used against him in the criminal proceedings. I've had plenty of time the last few months to watch TV."

Dr. Anton cleared his throat and looked at me. "Does this mean I'm done here today?"

"I guess so," I answered, still in a slight daze at the twist in events.

"Did you want to talk for a minute?" he asked. "I've canceled my morning to be here, so I have some time."

Having the opportunity to talk to a doctor witness without first writing a thousand-dollar check was not to be passed up.

"Can I buy you a cup of coffee?" I offered with a grin.

We walked down to the coffee shop in the courthouse. I paid for our coffees, and after he thanked me, he added, "Please, call me Angelo."

"Angelo, it is," I said, perhaps a little too gratefully. "I want to thank you for the report. It will go a long way in supporting Carol's version of the events when we talk to the people at Family Court Services and the judge. I hear you have been on the stand quite a bit." Better hair than me, handsome and trim and in a nice suit, he was every bit the professional.

He tilted his head in a deprecating nod and gave me a big smile. "It's California. Everybody wants to sue." Pause. "Automobiles—bad injuries." Pause. "Football, basketball, soccer—crazy injuries. You name it. Necks and backs aren't meant to be abused this way. And this guy, the husband...what could he have been thinking?"

"Sounds like the Budweiser was thinking for him. Tell me more about Carol's prognosis: now that the halo brace is off, when do you think she'll be able to lift her toddler, drive, go to work, return to a more normal life?"

"We'll have a better idea when we get her in later this week. She's doing physical therapy now. I'm thinking she could be driving after I see her again." He dug into his file and extracted Carol's first set of X-rays taken on February 10. "You see this tiny piece of white here," he said, pointing.

"Yes."

"That is a splinter of bone pressing against the sack that contains the spinal cord between C-2 and C-3. You can see, a millimeter or two more and she'd have had the cord infringed, maybe punctured. Any more than that and she'd have been a quadriplegic. Worst case, she'd have been on a ventilator the rest of her life."

I studied the X-rays a few moments more. "And now?"

"We'll know more when we get the next set. As to activities, even out of the halo collar, she'll still be on significant restrictions. I can't imagine her being able to lift more than eight pounds for a while. In addition to the bones continuing to heal, she has suffered some significant atrophy and stiffness in the muscles of her neck and may be subject to some serious headaches as she resumes movement. Physical therapy for another eight to twelve weeks. What a mean, stupid thing to do to someone!"

"You know that we may need you to testify in a civil case?"

"You mean divorce court or a personal injury case? You weren't sure when we talked on the phone."

I shrugged. "I'm still not certain. It could be both. For the time being, a good letter from you should be enough in the divorce case. We can have a vocational expert assess her situation based on your written report. You know, one expert relying on another expert. We aren't sure yet about filing an injury case, but it seems likely that we will."

"I'll be happy to write the report. I'll still have to charge, or my partners will be all over me, but it will be gentle." He paused. "I'm on the victim's side."

"We understand and appreciate your efforts, Angelo. We'll be in touch when we learn more. And we're all looking forward to Carol's recovery."

22 - More Criminal Charges?

May 7, 1985

The first thing I did when I got back to the office was to call ADA Novetsky. I wanted to find out about any pleas that were in the works that might undercut our chances to have something to enter into evidence. Frankly, I was surprised when he took my call.

"Mr. Gregory," he said. "What can I do for you?"

"Well," I replied, "I wanted to check in about this morning. Did you get the information from Rosa Hernandez about the other times Bill Collins raped Carol?"

"I did."

"Will you be adding to the charges?"

"At this point, we're only using them as leverage for a plea."

"About the plea. Carol, as the victim, is incurring a lot of medical expense and lost wages. It would be really a benefit to her if, as part of whatever gets done, that the plea is at least usable in the other proceedings that are going on."

"What do you mean?"

"Well, if he pleads guilty or nolo to a felony, you know that is admissible in civil court?"

"I'm aware of that."

"You're not considering a misdemeanor, are you?"

"Of course not. Not in this case."

I sighed with relief. "That is all I was worried about. Is there anything we can do to help the prosecution?"

"Not that I can think of. If something comes up, either Rosa or I will get back to you."

"One more thing. The psychologist, Dr. Gold, has made an application to the victim's fund for payment of her fees for treating Carol. Is there anything you can do to grease the wheels?"

"I'll have someone else in the office follow up on it."

"I appreciate that," I answered.

We ended the call, and I rounded my desk and poked my head into Marty's office. He and Jules were going over the calculations of the coefficient of friction on a slip-and-fall in a grocery store. They'd gone back to the office after the judge accepted the stipulation and I'd gone with Dr. Anton for coffee, so I filled them in on my conversations with Angelo and Plato.

Marty shook his head. "Something still doesn't pass the sniff test."

"Even the judge didn't like it, giving up on the prelim," Jules agreed. "But it sounds like Plato will hang in there for Carol."

I nodded. "Is there anyone you know at the DA's that can chase down the plea negotiations, Jules? I thought Rosa Hernandez would be a good source, but everything that happened today seemed like a surprise to her."

"Maybe. Let's give it a week and I'll check in."

We were talking about Michael Jordan's chances of being named NBA Rookie of the Year, when Sue poked her head in. "We just got Bill Collins' income and expense declaration."

23 - Bill's Income & Assets

May 7-13, 1985

Literally rolling up my shirt sleeves, I dug into the papers, an old-fashioned adding machine at my fingertips. I still hadn't gotten the hang of running spreadsheets on the newest piece of office equipment, a PC. And while I hated playing with numbers, it was part of the job. In every divorce case where there is a request for money, the parties must submit a Declaration of Income and Expense under penalty of perjury to speed the process for a judge to make calculations.

Fortunately a joint bench and bar committee had recently developed guideline formulas to help judges, and to smooth out the differences that frequently occurred with similar situations presented for decision. We had virtually no information on the Collins' family's income or expenses because it had all been handled by Bill; Carol wasn't working.

Bill's I&E showed no current income but acknowledged earning gross wages of almost $30,000 over the previous 12 months. In a footnote, he explained that he couldn't work now because of the stress from the criminal proceedings against him. The basic calculation gave him $2,200 per month in net income after taxes and required deductions, which seemed to me to be about right for his level of construction job. He had the usual living expenses, but two stood out: there was no car payment and he showed $880 for rent, representing exactly 40% of his net, which by itself seemed too coincidental to pass over. Additionally, Carol had said they were buying the house, not renting. From experience, the figure for rent seemed almost double what I'd expected.

In his schedule of Assets & Debts, he showed nothing for savings, pension, or other income. He didn't even list a car of his own, just the old '74 Ford Maverick that Carol drove. Carol's documents had listed her car and the household furniture and said all the other information was in Bill's possession. She did list a 1984 Ford F-150 truck that Bill drove and the house where they had been living on Vistamont Drive in San Jose as assets, though. There were a lot of questions for Bill's deposition.

24 - Motion for Support & Custody

May 14, 1985

I liked having my clients meet me at my office and then use the five-block walk to the family courthouse to calm their nerves while we went over last-minute items. That helped with Carol. Her simple blue dress literally hung on her, an indication of how much weight she'd lost since her injury. With a light camel jacket and flats on her feet, she seemed to perk up on the way over. She was chatty, but tense. And still wearing the soft collar.

She informed me she'd met with Dr. Anton last Friday. The X-rays showed good healing, but she would continue to be in a soft collar through the hearing. The bad news was she still couldn't drive a car since she couldn't easily turn her head. And even though her lifting limit had been raised to 15 pounds, she could not pick up Joey any time soon.

The courthouse devoted to divorce cases is a gray concrete, converted bank building at the corner of Almaden and Park. The courts refer to the building as "Park," but the protrusions bordering the entry stairs gave the front a resemblance to a Sphinx, which is what the lawyers called it. We climbed the stairs between the Sphinx' front legs to enter the courthouse. Although this courthouse was somewhat nicer than the Hall of Justice, it was no comparison to the functional finery of the Market Street courthouse. The drab concrete reflected the mood of despair for many of the clients passing through the security checkpoint, preparing them—or not—for what would happen to their lives next.

We were spilled into the huge main floor and assaulted by the sights and sounds of people, most of whom didn't want to be there, circling the central area of cubicles like a giant game of musical chairs, waiting to grab one for the meeting they really didn't want to have. I knew from first-hand experience that the cubicles provided only the illusion of privacy. The constant din in the background, coupled with an inability to see if anyone untoward was listening in to your private conversations from the other side of the cubicle wall, lulled you into mind-numbing acceptance of the environment. No matter. Many a time I defied reality and proceeded as if we were in a sound-proofed room, even as occasional screams and sobbing punctuated the grinding process. Profanities were muttered as files slipped off lawyers' thighs and scattered on the floor. Depression reigned. "No way!" is perhaps one of the nicest shouts I heard echoing off the hard walls and ceiling.

Standing next to me, Carol gripped my elbow and stared at the chaotic setting. In preparing clients for the Motions Calendar and trial, we try to have them come to court weeks before they are scheduled to witness how things actually worked. It's certainly nothing like television. I'd suggested that to Carol but there was no one to drive her there and sit with her while she took it all in. Her mother still wasn't that supportive, her father wasn't in a position to take the time off work, and Jill—my first suggestion—somehow didn't seem to be available. Nevertheless, her mother had dropped Carol at my office, on time. Carol was to call her mother when she was ready to be picked up.

In the meantime, I stashed Carol in the quietest corner I could find, and headed into the courtroom.

Judge DePalma was on the motion calendar. His process was to run through all the cases listed to take the shortest matters first, and no estimate on the morning "short cause" calendar could exceed 30 minutes. This always led to gentle misrepresentation by the attorneys. It was kind of like the old TV show where contestants competed for the chance to name a tune in the fewest notes. To discourage that in his courtroom, Judge DePalma's bailiff would set a timer to track the time each side took and matched it to their estimates. If they were out of time, they had to wait until the end of the calendar to finish.

Don and I each estimated 10 minutes for our presentations, including cross-examination. This put us out of the courtroom until after the morning break, about 10:30 a.m.

Don showed no interest in reaching any kind of settlement.

"No can do. Bill's out of work," he answered when I asked flat out. "There's no income on which to base support."

"But he has the ability to earn $30K a year," I countered, "so the judge can impute that income."

"I don't think he will in this case, especially at a temporary hearing."

"What about child sharing? Can we set up a schedule?" I wanted to develop something that wouldn't eat into my precious 10 minutes with the judge.

"Family Court Services," Don responded.

I was mad at Don's recalcitrance. That meant Family Court Services would have to interview both Bill and Carol, maybe see Joey, and finally do an evaluation.

"That could be months!" I objected. "And you know that FCS has been coming down on parents who deny access."

"We're not denying access. We know Carol can't chase after a toddler and we're doing what we can for her to see Joey when she has help to care for him."

"Will you at least tell me where he's getting the money to pay the rent?" I spit out.

Don answered in his most sincere voice, "He's borrowing from his father."

I had to walk away in frustration.

At 10:45 a.m., the bailiff stuck his head out of the courtroom and called for the remaining cases for Department 14. Judge DePalma called us first. After moving to the presentation tables with our clients and stating our appearances, he asked, "Have you come to any agreements that might help make this case move along?"

It was our motion, so I was expected to begin. "No, Your Honor. But it looks like we'll need an emergency referral to Family Court Services. We couldn't get any agreements on support, visitation or custody."

"I don't think it needs to be an emergency," Don chimed in. "Mrs. Collins has been unable to physically handle their active child and we have made him available when she's had help."

"So far, she's only had five days in the last two and a half months," I responded. "With no agreement for a schedule that would even provide a chance to arrange help."

The judge held up a hand, signaling us to stop. "I'll grant the emergency referral. What about support and attorney fees? Give me a moment while I look at your declarations."

Don and I knew enough to be quiet while the judge was reading. After a minute or two, he looked at Don and asked, "How is Mr. Collins paying his rent?"

"He's borrowing from his father," Don answered.

Judge DePalma turned to me. "Is Mrs. Collins planning to leave her parents' home any time soon?"

"As soon as she is able, Your Honor. She's recently had the metal halo that was stabilizing her neck removed, but is still in a soft collar. She'd very much like to be able to get her own apartment as soon as she has sufficient funds available. The budget we presented shows she'd have about $1,500 per month minimum in expenses on her own. We still need some idea of visitation and custody to know how that would be affected by Joey. We believe that Mr. Collins has voluntarily made himself unemployed—"

"There is no basis for that allegation!" Don interrupted. "Your Honor is aware, is he not, that criminal proceedings have begun and—"

Judge DePalma held up his hand again, stopping Don cold. I bit back my heated retort.

"Is the criminal case set for trial?" the judge asked.

Don shook his head. "Not yet, Your Honor. Mr. Collins has pleaded not guilty and we are awaiting a trial date."

"Wasn't one set at the prelim?" Judge DePalma appeared surprised.

"No." Again, Don shook his head.

"But the judge at the prelim found sufficient evidence to warrant a trial, didn't he?"

"The DA and defense counsel stipulated to sufficient evidence. There was no hearing, per se." At least Don had the grace to look contrite.

The judge's eyebrows shot up. "I've never seen that." He caught himself, surely aware that it was just as surprising for him to make his last statement out loud and on the record. With a long pause and short cough, he continued. "Is there a stipulation that the matters represented here by counsel today would have been the testimony of the parties, had they been called to the stand?" That was our cue to shut up or incur his wrath.

"Yes, Your Honor," we both said.

"Very well, then. I'm going to order this matter to Family Court Services for emergency screening as to custody and visitation. You are to report directly there when we finish this hearing. Also, I'm going to reserve jurisdiction over Mr. Gregory's request for fees and the application for support. I'm prepared to make the support retroactive to..." he checked his file, "April 5th, the date the motion was filed. I want you all back here on May 23rd." He bent over the bench and whispered with his clerk, then announced, "Make that May 24th at 1:30. Please let FCS know to have the screening report to me well before then. Anything further, gentlemen?"

There was only one response. "No, Your Honor."

I picked up the referral slip from the bailiff and we left the courtroom.

* * * * *

"Was this good or bad?" Harris asked. "I mean, what is a reservation of jurisdiction for support, anyway? Doesn't that just mean she's stuck at her mom's house?"

I smiled. "You're paying attention! It really means that when he goes back to work a judge can tally up all the support that would have been paid and see if there is a way to move some money to Carol. If they don't reserve jurisdiction to a specific date, Bill could go to work the next day and not owe anything. This is one way to protect the needy spouse."

25 - Family Court Services' Kathryn Monahan

May 14, 1985

FCS was on the second floor of the courthouse. Don and Bill climbed the stairs, Don obviously filling Bill in on the situation. I waited at the elevator with Carol, explaining what would be happening next. Entering the FCS office, I gave the judge's referral slip to the receptionist and leaned closer so Carol couldn't hear me.

"We'll need either Sandy or Kathryn on this one," I whispered to her. "It's going to be difficult."

"They are both meeting with clients now," the receptionist replied. "But one of them will break free soon. If you don't mind waiting about 20 minutes, I'll hold it until then."

"Twenty minutes? If that's all, we'll be thrilled." Relieved, I escorted Carol to the waiting area, careful to put distance between her and Bill.

Thankfully, we had to wait only 15 minutes before Kathryn Monahan appeared in front of us. Kathryn was a Licensed Clinical Social Worker with 10 years' experience doing custody and visitation evaluations for the court. Her warm, inviting smile disarmed almost any uptight parent. She knew what she was doing and was beloved in the community.

"Mr. Gregory, Mr. Fraser, won't you come in?" I wasn't surprised she maintained her formal, professional demeanor in front of the parties until she knew more of the situation.

Two metal client chairs were arranged in front of her tiny desk. Don and I sat.

Kathryn looked at me and said, "In 60 seconds or less, what's going on?"

"This is a case of extreme domestic violence. In February, dad broke mom's neck while he was trying to rape her. She has been incapacitated in a fixed-head stabilization device—called a halo—until a few weeks ago. Dad was arrested and his parents took control of their now 21-month-old infant. Mom hasn't been given the chance to spend any real time with the kid and wants custody."

She turned to Don. "Your turn."

"Mom is a pathological liar who made up the whole rape story," Don stated. "She is incapable both mentally and physically of taking care of their child."

"Well, it looks like you guys are trying to make this easy for me." Kathryn smiled. "Since your stories don't match at all, we'll have to interview each of them, and maybe the child." She paused a moment. "But the child interview will be more about observation than anything else, given his age. I see that you're back in court in 10 days, so let's get out the calendars. I don't have time today to interview the parties in any depth, but I'd like to spend about 5-10 minutes with each of them now, and then see them separately. I have time Thursday, day after tomorrow. Who wants Thursday at 9:30 and who wants 1:30?"

"We'd like Carol to come in at 9:30," I jumped in before Don could answer. I knew that would be the easiest time for her to get a ride from Jill.

"Then I guess we'll take the 1:30," said Don. "Which of them do you want to see first today?"

"I may as well start with Carol."

Fifteen minutes later, Carol and I were walking back to my office. Carol carried some forms Kathryn had given her to complete and return the day after tomorrow.

"Will you help me fill these papers out?" Carol's voice carried tones of uncertainty.

Rather than give a direct answer, I asked, "When are you seeing Dr. Gold again?"

"Tomorrow. At 11."

"Great. I want to talk to her about getting you prepared for the longer interview with Kathryn. The forms are more effective if they are in your words, not mine. But I will want to talk with you before you submit them on Thursday. Let's get some time scheduled when we get to the office."

26 - Carol's Custody Readiness & Other Lies

May 14, 1985

A few minutes later, we got off the elevator and went into our suite. First, I asked Sue about our calendar the next day and settled on a 2:30 p.m. phone conference with Carol. Then Carol came into my office and I called Dr. Gold. Thankfully, she was available.

"Dr. Gold, I'm here with Carol Collins," I began. "She tells me you have an appointment together tomorrow at 11 o'clock. Is that correct?"

"Yes. Is there something specific you want us to work on?"

"She has paperwork to fill out for FCS before her meeting with Kathryn Monahan on Thursday morning. She is going to have some questions, but I think the best thing would be for you to work with her on her responses to the obvious questions she'll be asked in the interview."

"That's great that we've got Kathryn. Is there anything specific you are anticipating as a problem area?"

"That's why I wanted to have you on the phone as I explain it to Carol." I took a deep breath, keeping a careful eye on Carol's face. "Bill's attorney says that Carol is neither mentally, nor physically, capable of caring for Joey on her own. He says that Carol has a history of accusing Bill of dastardly deeds and that he has never physically harmed her in any way."

Carol gasped. "That liar!" she shouted.

"Put me on the speaker," Diane said.

I pressed the speaker button. "Go ahead, Diane. Carol can hear you now."

"Carol, we've talked about this possibility. We have worked on your history with Bill, and we'll go over it again tomorrow and get you ready. OK?"

Carol started to nod, then winced from the neck pain.

"She's got it," I answered for her. "And this will be a good warm-up for when she has to appear for depositions. You'll work on her breathing exercises as well as the actual answers?"

"Of course."

"Carol and I have a telephone appointment at 2:30 tomorrow. Will you be able to check in with me before then?"

"I'll probably have about 10 minutes to return calls between 1:50 and 2, so it'll be tight, but we'll get it done."

"Talk to you then." I hung up.

I met Carol's dismayed gaze. "OK," I said in what I hoped was a reassuring voice. "You'll be working with Dr. Gold tomorrow. Let's go over what's likely to happen." We spent the next quarter hour laying out the sequence of events and logistics for the next two days, then she left. I still was worried about her capacity to advocate for herself.

Working on other cases that afternoon, it seemed like nothing fit, so I went home early. When I walked in the door, Sarah took one look at me and said she'd take me for a cool-down walk.

27 - Obstacles

May 15, 1985

At 1:55 p.m. the next day, Diane called. Without preamble, she stated, "Carol's a whole lot better than when we started a month ago, but today she was really shaky. The ups and downs are expected, but timing is unpredictable. I reassured her that Kathryn is not there to twist her words or undermine her in any way. I helped her with her answers to Bill's accusation that she's the liar; her own history of Bill's abuse, both physical and mental; and her limitations in caring for Joey. I think this is going to be a gradual process because of Joey's young age and the minimal time he's had with Carol in the last few months. Other than that, it's all we can do for now. Gotta run. Bye."

I barely had time to say, "Goodbye," before I heard her phone click. But I'd heard from her.

As promised, I called Carol at 2:30 p.m. When she picked up, her voice was wobbly and rough as she said hello, like she'd been crying.

"Carol, I'm sorry you're struggling so much," I said. "What can I do to help?"

"I wish I knew." She sobbed some more.

"Well, here's the deal. Tomorrow you are going to deliver your forms to Kathryn. Then she's going to take a few minutes and ask you some questions. She's not there to trick you or make you feel bad. You went over this with Dr. Gold, didn't you?"

"Yes, but I still don't feel ready."

"OK, what's bothering you?"

"That he says I lie and that I can't take care of Joey."

"What does it take to take care of Joey that gives you trouble?"

"Well, he's still in diapers and I can't lift him onto the changing table. He still sleeps in a crib and I can't lift him into the crib. I can't bend over the tub to bathe him. I can't lift him to give him hugs. It goes on and on."

"What can you do?"

"I can feed him, talk with him, read to him, sit by him. I can hug him when we are sitting on the couch together."

"If he is with you overnight at your parent's house, where would he sleep?"

"They set up a playroom with a crib. The house has five bedrooms, one they call the playroom. They've set up another bedroom for me. I've been there for over two months now, since I got out of the hospital."

"I remember. It's very nice. Has Joey spent the night?"

"Twice."

"And he survived?"

"Yes, he did fine!" Her voice lightened, as if a light bulb went off in her brain. "My parents helped before and after work and Jill stopped by a couple of times to help me change diapers."

"Will those people still help?"

"Yes!"

"And how much longer before you can lift him?"

"He's about 40 pounds now. It could be another six months." She seemed calmer now, and not as depressed.

"Well, be honest with Kathryn. Don't overstate your capabilities with Joey and she'll know you are truthful. She's no dummy. She's seen thousands of families. My guess is that she'll start giving you more and more time as long as there are other people to help you, and then even more time when you don't need the help as Joey adapts to your abilities."

We went through the forms and she promised to stop by tomorrow after her meeting with Kathryn.

28 - Carol's Response to Initial Success

May 16, 1985

When I saw her the next day, Carol was as cheerful as I'd ever seen her. She actually smiled as she held out her hand to shake mine.

"You were right," she admitted. "Kathryn *is* a nice lady. I think she really wants to help. I talked to her about the things I can do now and the things I still need help with. She seemed to understand and explained that she wants to get me as much time with Joey as possible, as soon as possible, but she can't just take him completely away from Bill. She needs to talk with Bill before she can make any decisions."

"Did the lying come up?" I couldn't help from asking.

"You were right about that, too." Carol flashed a broad, genuine smile. "She said she liked the way I answered questions about Joey honestly. She did ask if there were other times when Bill was violent to me. I started to list a couple of times that I'd talked about with Dr. Gold and she stopped me. She said I didn't have to go through it all again; she believed me."

"Well then, all we have to do is wait for a report. Just be ready to accept that this will all be done in stages."

"I will. Thank you again." We shook hands once more, and her grip was perceptibly firmer.

Later than afternoon, when I returned to my desk from another court hearing, a vase of flowers sat plopped in the middle.

Uh-oh, I thought. Did I forget a family birthday? A moment of panic—Sarah's? Our anniversary?

I retrieved the card nestled in the arrangement, delivered by The Downtown Florist, located two blocks from our office. It read: "From a secret admirer."

* * * * *

Harris asked, "Did you ever find out who sent them?"

"Well," I started, "we called the florist and found out that whoever had sent them had been insistent that they do not tell me who sent them. I'd guessed it was Carol but wasn't sure. The card was in the handwriting of someone from the shop."

"But you found out later, didn't you?"

"Yes," I said. "But the point wasn't whether Carol had sent them. The question was, what did it mean? We can guess that she had a crush on me. Has that happened to you? That you found out that a girl had a crush on you?"

He blushed. "It's happened a few times."

"And what happened?"

"In junior high a girl I didn't even know had a friend talk to a friend of mine and we wound up going to the movies. Not much. We texted back and forth for a while, but I guess I wasn't that interested."

I nodded at him. "And in high school?"

His blush deepened. "As a freshman, a girl I hardly knew asked me to her Junior Prom." When I just waited, he continued, "And then we dated for a few months." Harris seemed to have inherited his father's reticence to talk, and quite willing to wait me out.

"OK, Harris. Did you go out with her because you were flattered or because you liked her from the start?"

"At first, um, I guess it was really flattering and exciting to go out with an upperclassman. But then I got to know more girls from my class and started to like one of them."

"Do you think that dating the junior made you more attractive to the other freshmen?"

"Probably," he said.

"Did you treat them the same—that is, romantically?" I wasn't ready to start having a conversation with my grandson about sex and the differences between freshmen and juniors.

"Sort of," he stammered, then deflected. "But let's get back to your story."

I struggled with the words to tell him about being careful and treating his dates with respect, but couldn't come up with a way to do it, leaving it for his parents. "OK. Let's have a talk after we get to my conversation with Dr. Gold. In the meantime, just think about all the bonus points I got when I brought the flowers home to Grandma Sarah." I didn't tell him that Sarah always complained I never gave her flowers.

29 - Report from Family Court Services

May 22, 1985

Kathryn Monahan's report, which I received on the Wednesday before the hearing, translated into my words was basically this: "Bill Collins is a lying scumbag who beats and rapes his wife. Carol Collins can barely care for herself, let alone a child in diapers." Tell me something I didn't know. At least she recommended that Joey spend an increasing amount of time with Carol, including overnights, with frequent check-ins on her status and capacity to handle additional time with Joey. And she said there was no evidence that Bill had been directly violent with Joey.

I faxed a copy to Dr. Gold and asked her to call me as soon as she'd read it.

Diane called about an hour later. "Isn't that pretty much what I told you weeks ago?"

"I know. And I get that this is probably the only sensible solution short of giving custody to Carol's parents. I'm not sure which solution would be better for Joey over the next six months."

"Frankly, I think putting Carol's parents in charge would be even more difficult for Carol. I'd love to be able to evaluate all the parties at this dance, but we know that's not going to happen."

"Is Carol ready for this recommendation?"

"I think so."

With only the slightest hesitation, I told her about the flowers. "Is that something Carol would do?"

"We've known there is some transference building up. You know, when she comes to depend on you as more than just her concerned, caring lawyer. And she thinks you're doing this because of your attraction to her."

"How do I stop it?"

"Continue to maintain your boundaries. Be professional. Don't get seduced by her vulnerability. Don't get naked with her." She giggled.

"That was unprofessional," I said, smiling to myself.

"The statement or the giggle?"

"Both."

30 - Harris Introduced to Transference

July 9, 2016

"Now?" Harris cajoled.

"Now. You know that transference is when someone takes a memory from another time or relationship and attributes that feeling to a new situation with someone else?" He nodded and I went on, "If Carol had dated someone who treated her with respect and listened to her with some empathy, she might well transfer that attraction to someone else who treated her the same way. Therapists, lawyers, even doctors must be prepared to deal with transference to one degree or another. Some professionals deal with it by being cold and distant. Some don't understand the dynamic and respond inappropriately. In fact, the legal canons of ethics prohibit lawyers from having a sexual relationship with a client, otherwise they can lose their license. I have known a few lawyers who were suspended and even disbarred for having sex with a client."

"How do you know if it is this transference or a real case of love?"

"You're right. There may not be a good way to tell, which is why Diane said for me to maintain my boundaries. That means, besides her tongue-in-cheek advice about not getting naked with her, that I have to continue to play my role as the attorney-advocate, not as a date or lover."

"What was that like for you? I mean, didn't it just feel weird?"

"Yes, it did, but it also felt right. I discovered I have an innate mindset to rescue someone in trouble, and that probably clouded my thinking somewhat. That's easy for me to say now, but I didn't recognize it at the time, certainly." I paused, considering all the facts again. "Actually, in hindsight, I wonder if Diane knew that about me and, in her own subtle way, played on my need to rescue Carol as a way to keep me dogged and persistent in all the ups and downs of the case for Carol's sake."

"Sounds like Dr. D cared a lot about Carol."

"She always did—Carol and me, too. That's why she warned me to be careful. She and I both knew it would have been very easy to take advantage of Carol emotionally or even sexually, but totally wrong. Besides, I was and am happy with Grandma Sarah. OK?"

As if on cue, Sarah came to find us. "Are you guys ready for some lunch?"

"You know I'm always ready to eat!" Harris jumped up from his chair. As we were making sandwiches from the spread Sarah had put out for us, she asked, "Where are you in the story?"

"You just got some flowers," I said with a wink.

"And Grandpa was telling me about transference," Harris added.

"Has he gotten to the Drama Triangle yet?"

"No," I said. "I'm saving that for later. Are you OK if we take our food out to the patio and keep going?"

"So when am I going to get some time with my grandson?" Sarah crossed her arms across her chest and scowled, probably only half in jest.

"At the rate we're going, it should be dinner." I turned to Harris. "Would you like to stay for dinner?"

"Yup. Let's keep going."

He didn't even ask what we were having.

31 - A Decision on Support & Fees

On Friday, we all showed up at Judge DePalma's court at 1:30 p.m., including Kathryn. The judge came down off the bench to the area beside the parties' tables and pulled up a chair. He directed the bailiff to close the door to the courtroom so we wouldn't be disturbed.

Judge DePalma glanced at the papers in front of him. "You've all seen the report. We have Ms. Monahan here to help us work through a temporary sharing arrangement. Ms. Monahan, please proceed."

Despite the judge's instructions, unbelievably Don spoke up first. "Clearly, Carol cannot be left alone with Joey if she can't even lift him to change a diaper by herself. And, God forbid, if he had any kind of medical problem, she couldn't even drive him to the doctor's office or a hospital."

Rather than piss off the judge, I stayed quiet and let Kathryn handle it.

Fortunately, Kathryn remained calm. "Sad, but mostly true," she said. "But there are plenty of times when there are others in the house or nearby who can fulfill those duties. It is important that Joey spend as much time with her as possible. And she can still dial a phone."

"How would you make the visitation happen?" Judge DePalma asked her.

"From what I've gathered, Carol's father works a pretty regular work week," Kathryn replied. "Her mom's hours as a realtor are flexible, so she could be there as back-up in the mornings, but I'd like to talk further with all of the grandparents to help work out a schedule. Unless the lawyers here think they can do it."

I figured that was my cue, so I jumped in. "We recognize that Carol is not ready to be a full-time primary caretaker, but we can make sure there is coverage three to four days a week. If we did that for another month or six weeks, we could see how Carol is improving, and then be in touch with Ms. Monahan to help us re-work the schedule if it is appropriate to add time."

Don glared at me. "What you are proposing now is essentially a jump to 50-50, with an expectation of more. We oppose that. We contend that Carol is also psychologically incapable of being a primary parent and intend to prove that at trial."

The judge looked at Kathryn. "Do you believe Mrs. Collins Is psychologically incapable of being a primary parent?"

"If she were without any support people, that might, and I emphasize might, be the case. But this plan would have support people in place."

"Will we have the opportunity to vet the support people?" Don asked.

"I'll be happy to interview *all* of the grandparents," Kathryn replied, with a sweet smile. "Would that make you happy?"

"Actually, it would. I think you'll be very impressed with Thomas and Mary Collins," Don added. "Less so with Mr. and Mrs. Polansky."

"OK," said the judge. "Mr. Gregory, will you prepare a temporary Order of the Court for a three-day, four-day time share, with a maternal grandparent or other responsible adult to be available whenever your client has the child. It should also have all of the grandparents scheduled to meet with Ms. Monahan by..." He looked at Kathryn.

"Give me three weeks, please," Kathryn requested. "Will It be OK to do this by telephone?"

"Of course," said the judge. "How's June 12th for a return to this court?"

We all nodded. The Clerk said he had an hour at 2:30 p.m. that day, and we all agreed to return. Kathryn gathered up her papers and briefcase and exited the room.

I wasn't yet ready to leave. "Your Honor? We still have the matter of support and attorney fees."

"I recall," he said. "$1,225 per month temporary family support, retroactive to April 5th, 1985. Subject to review again on June 12th. $2,500 for interim attorney's fees. I expect all arrears to be paid by June 1st, including the payment for June, along with the fees."

"Your Honor, Mr. Collins is not even working!" Don could barely stop sputtering.

"He clearly has the ability to borrow to keep his own household afloat. We can sort out any debts incurred later in the case." Although he was kicking the can down the road, I liked the judge's approach.

"Your Honor," I began, "before we leave, I'd like to follow up about depositions. Don, can we set a date before June 12th when you can do two hours with Carol and I can do two hours with Bill? With a good break in between?"

Don turned to the judge. "Are you going to limit the time this way? The Code of Civil Procedure gives me the right to finish my questioning before Mr. Gregory begins."

"The report from Ms. Monahan was pretty clear about Mrs. Collins current abilities," Judge DePalma responded quickly. "I think I have the discretion to let you start, but not drag it out to the point that it winds up denying Mr. Gregory the ability to engage in effective advocacy. I think the proposal of equal time makes sense under the circumstances. If you can't make headway and come back to me, I'll appoint a discovery master. Anything else, gentlemen?"

I faced Don. "When will we get the documents we requested?"

"By Tuesday, the 28th," came his terse answer.

I turned back to the judge. "Nothing further from me. Thank you, Your Honor."

Don thanked the judge as well and we stopped in the hallway to compare calendars for depositions, settling on Monday, June 10.

32 - Talking About Domestic Violence & Child Sharing

July 9, 2016

"I'm still confused about why someone like Bill could share parenting responsibilities the way it was done," Harris remarked, dismay marring his young features. "Weren't you mad at Kathryn and the judge? I mean, Bill seems like a terrible person and Carol loses out because she can't do some things?"

"Harris," I said, "the law has changed since then. Now it is recognized that violence by one parent against the other is presumed to be violence against the child or children, and there is a presumption that the violent parent should not have custody. In fact, with a history like this, today Bill would probably not even have visitation without a neutral supervisor present."

That settled him down a bit, but he continued to vent his frustration at the lying that seemed to be a big part of what the legal business was about.

"Well," I said, "I don't think any business can count on all of the people that work there being 100% truthful 100% of the time. How many employees has your Uncle had to fire from his McDonald's restaurants because of lying or stealing?"

"I don't know, but it does happen," he admitted.

"Have any of your friends been caught cheating on a school exam?"

He cringed. "My friend Sean got caught with some math formulas written on his sock and was suspended for two weeks. But that doesn't seem anywhere near the same as what this Bill guy did to Carol."

"I know. But remember that I told you that is one of the big reasons we're talking about this case and not one that went smoothly. That is why it is my most memorable. In almost any career you choose, you are going to have to deal with conflict. Doctors work under pressure and must deal with interference from patients' families and even competition with colleagues. Within the corporate structure, people are trying to get ahead of co-workers for raises and promotions. And politics…don't get me started."

"It sounds like you got something for Carol on the support and fees to make you happy. So why don't you sound satisfied with that result?"

"Yes, I got some of the fees. It was a start that I think served as a warning to Don. You remember my conversations earlier about Don doing what he could to delay us and make us work for everything? How that made his client happy and got Don paid?"

"So all his bullshit was about the money?"

"A lot of it, but it was also positioning for the criminal case. He didn't want Bill to be subject to any questioning that might jeopardize him in the criminal indictment. But we still have a long way to go in the story before you'll understand it all."

33 - Meeting with Dr. D & Lunch with Carol

May 28, 1985

I called Carol, eager to begin our preparation for the upcoming depositions. With only 10 days to go, we had a lot to do. I explained to her that Don would have the chance to question her and that I would be at her side to protect her from any verbal abuse by Bill or his attorney. I also explained that she would be sworn in by a certified court reporter who would use a transcription machine just like the one she'd seen in the courtroom. Don would have the transcript of what was said and would be able to use the transcript to contradict any statements made by her during cross-examination in court if they were different. I would be able to do the same with Bill. We arranged for a session that Friday at Diane's office, feeling that Carol would be most comfortable in that environment.

When I arrived, Diane delayed me for a minute in the waiting room. "Carol is extremely embarrassed about her history of abuse," Diane warned, "but she knows that explaining it all is necessary. Even though she knows you have to be present, she won't be able to look at you while she tells her story. I'll keep her moving through it as chronologically as I can, so just stay quiet. I'll tell you when you can start questions. OK?"

"I'll play it your way, but will she be able to withstand a deposition without you there?"

She shrugged. "Let's see how she does today, then make a decision."

Diane's office was cozy. The walls were a pinkish gray, a color meant to be calming. There was an overstuffed sofa against one wall, two upholstered chairs, with doilies on the arms to cover the sweat stains. The top three shelves of a bookcase were crammed with reference volumes; toys and games were stacked on the bottom two shelves. There was a child's sand tray in one corner and Diane's desk was tucked across the room. Arranged on the walls were framed prints in soothing, abstract colors. No Rorschach inkblots.

Carol was settled in one of the overstuffed chairs that had been turned to face an abstract print with more pinks and grays. She still wore the soft collar neck support, but had graduated to a button-up top and slacks—not sweats.

Diane closed the door behind us and steered me to the left. "Carol, Steve is here and is going to sit on the couch while you and I go through the history we've been working on. He will have some questions when we are done. Are you ready?"

I could barely hear Carol when she began to talk. Diane had to prompt her to start over, reminding her to speak up some more. Carol held a squeeze ball that she shifted from hand to hand.

"Bill and I met at a bar in Los Gatos," Carol started, haltingly. "I think it was Carrie Nation's. It was probably a Saturday night in spring or early summer of 1982. I was with Jill. Bill bought me a drink and came over to talk to us. He seemed nice. He stayed with us for a while and offered to take me home. I told Jill it was OK for her to go ahead—her husband, Tony would be expecting her—and I'd let Bill take me home."

She sipped some water and paused for a moment. Diane asked her what happened when Bill took her home.

"We'd both had a few drinks and, um, we made out for a while, but he was a gentleman and took 'no' for an answer. It was about two in the morning when I got back to my apartment."

Diane prompted her to state where her apartment was and Carol gave an address on Moorpark, not too far from San Jose City Junior College. They digressed for a while and Carol talked about working toward an Associate Degree in business from the JC and working as a cashier at a gas station for a little over minimum wage. There was a progression in the relationship with Bill and she became pregnant in November or December 1982. Bill told Carol he was happy that she was pregnant, and proposed as soon as he heard. They were married March 26, 1983, over the objections of her mother who didn't think Bill was good enough for Carol. They went to Disneyland for their honeymoon.

Retelling these mundane details seemed to relax Carol a bit. Shooting a glance at me, Diane asked Carol when Bill was first violent with her.

"It was on our honeymoon. We had been in the park all day and got back to the hotel about 11 o'clock that night. I was exhausted and queasy from the pregnancy and exertion. My feet hurt. My back hurt. Bill wanted to have sex as soon as we got to the room. I asked him to maybe wait until morning, before we planned to go back into the park. He pushed me onto the bed and said he wanted to 'do it now' and started pulling off my shorts. When I said 'no,' he said, 'Yes, now, or I'll punch you in the belly!' I started crying but he pulled off my shorts and had sex with me anyway. It hurt."

Diane very gently took her through a multitude of acts of violent sex leading up to the attack in February 1985. There was an escalation until he no longer allowed her to wear a nightgown. If she did, he'd tear it off of her. He never broke any bones or left a visible bruise. Occasionally he would apologize and bring her flowers, but there was virtually no foreplay or wooing behavior.

Well aware that this meeting was to prepare Carol for her deposition, Diane asked the question for me, the one that would be on the minds of the judge and jury. "Carol, why didn't you leave him?"

"First I was pregnant, me and my mom hadn't talked in months—she hated Bill. I'd left my job at the gas station just before Joey was born and didn't go back to work. So I had no money and nowhere to go! I couldn't just move out with Joey and still take care of him. I was really stuck."

It was clear to me that she was being truthful and would be a good witness, but it was going to be difficult for her to testify. I'd heard similar responses from other clients, but there was something in the way Carol spoke that I believed would resonate with a judge and jury. Her very posture and quavering voice were genuine proof of her PTSD. I didn't think she was capable of acting the emotions on display, but made a mental note to ask Diane if that were possible.

Diane walked Carol through a few more incidents, then a retelling of the night her neck was injured. I passed Diane a note that I thought this was enough about the relationship for today, but to have her talk about the house on Vistamont; why did she think it was theirs?

Looking relieved at the respite, Carol explained that when they got married, Bill had told her that his dad had loaned him the money for a down payment when he moved in, sometime in

1980. She remembered signing some papers about the house, but couldn't remember exactly what they were.

By now, Carol was pretty worn down. Diane said she had to kick us out to get ready for her next client. I reminded Diane we needed to touch base again soon to decide about the need for her to be at the depositions on June 10, and asked if Carol would like to join me at the Mexican restaurant next door for some lunch before heading home. Diane encouraged Carol to go, saying it would help her become more comfortable around me as we prepared for her deposition and court.

Before leaving, I had Carol go out to the waiting room while I asked Diane whether Carol was capable of acting in her depictions of the relationship with Bill. She gave me a look that could stop a rhino. "Not possible!" was all she said.

After we were seated in the restaurant and had ordered, I asked Carol how things were going with Joey. She brightened.

"Well, I can't lift him up yet; that is probably a month or so away. But I am seeing him a couple days a week and my parents have been a big help. We've even had him overnight." She explained how Diane had helped her with her relationship with her parents, how she was looking forward to getting better, and even going back to work.

I described more about the upcoming deposition and rules for answering questions: first, listen carefully to the question; second, answer only the question, and if you don't understand the question, just say so; third, don't guess; and fourth, tell the truth. I even quoted Mark Twain: "There's less to remember when you just tell the truth."

Lunch arrived and we started to eat. I felt something on my leg. It took me a moment to realize what was happening. Carol had slipped off her shoe and was rubbing her foot on my calf. I looked up and caught her staring at me with a very shy smile and a question in her eyes. She looked as vulnerable as a five-year-old child. But it wasn't a five-year-old's smile. Tempting as it was, my conscience prevailed. I couldn't think of anything to say that wouldn't embarrass both of us. I gently shook my head and shifted my leg away.

I led the conversation instead into the actual questions that would come up during depositions regarding sharing Joey and their financial division, and asked if she needed Diane to be there for the deposition. She said she would be OK if Diane was not there. We said goodbye in the parking lot and shook hands.

* * * * *

The next morning I received a flower arrangement with a cryptic card reading: *"message had to be censored."* There was no signature.

Later that day I was able to get ahold of Diane, and told her what had happened at lunch and the flowers with the censored message.

"Thanks for letting me know," she sighed. "We talked about this when you got the first batch of flowers. I was afraid her feelings might escalate. I think this is still a product of transference. Pretty much full-blown. Good work on setting your boundaries and not calling her out on the spot. I'll have another talk with her about her boundaries. Just remember that offering herself sexually is her way of surviving, of coping in an uncertain situation." I was glad Diane hadn't giggled again, cute as it was.

When I got home that evening, Sarah lit up at the sight of the flower arrangement. "It looks like we'll both get lucky tonight," she said with a wink.

34 - More About Transference

July 9, 2016

Harris was intrigued. "We just talked about transference, but I don't get how that is going to make some young woman make a pass at an old guy like you!"

He made me laugh. "Looks like I have your attention. Remember we were all younger in 1986. She was 28 and I was close to 40. Don't get me wrong; it is flattering and I don't know anyone who doesn't like to be flattered. There are going to be many temptations in your life: sex, money, alcohol, drugs, power over others. How we deal with those is as much a matter of ethics and your conscience as it is about obeying the law. How I would feel about cheating on Grandma—she wasn't a grandma then, although I still think she's pretty hot—for a moment of sexual gratification? I think she might have given me a pass if it were Jennifer Aniston—"

"Who?"

I chuckled again. "Haven't you seen the TV sit-com *Friends?* Just think of whoever a hottie is for your generation, someone like that. But we both know that I'd have a better chance of winning the lottery."

He grinned, a very masculine, knowing grin, but didn't dispute my conclusion. He was growing up fast, too fast.

"As I told you earlier," I continued, "it is very common for clients and patients to believe that a caring way of listening is the sign of a deeper relationship, sometimes even erotic."

"Awkward!"

"Yes, it is. That's why it's great to have someone like Diane working on the case. She can use this transference concept to start working with the client to help her understand what healthy attachment is, especially in professional relationships. Increasing her self-awareness in this context will, hopefully, help prepare her for healthy relationships in other aspects of her life."

"So, did Diane get things straightened out with Carol?"

"Maybe. I hoped so. I didn't know. But there were other problems that we'll talk about later."

"OK. What happened next?"

"Do you remember when we went to court in April and got some protective orders about depositions?"

"Wasn't that when you were going to start asking Carol's husband about what he did to her?"

Smart kid, I thought. He's actually tracking the story and not just killing time. "That's it. Remember there were problems with scheduling, and Don kept holding up the criminal proceedings as a barrier to Bill answering any of my obvious questions. Anyway, we finally got the depositions scheduled with Carol in the morning and Bill in the afternoon."

35 - Carol's Deposition

June 10, 1985

I met Carol in the lobby of a tall office building in the Pruneyard, the shopping-office complex in Campbell on Bascom Avenue. We took the elevator to Don's office and were directed to their conference room. Carol was nervous, but we'd spent enough time that she knew what was going to happen. She was still wearing the soft collar, more for comfort than need. Today she wore a sleeveless blouse and had a light sweater over her arm which she put on as soon as the air conditioning in Don's office hit us.

The conference room had a windowed wall facing the beautiful foothills on the east side of the valley. My own office had a similar view, one I thought of as the best in Silicon Valley. It was a typically gorgeous June day, hot and sunny, but with wispy clouds leaving shadows to decorate the foothills which exhibited their mid-summer tan. Don's first trick was an old one. His conference seating arrangement was already in place, with a court reporter at one end and Don set up adjacent to the reporter on the long edge of the table with his back to the bright view, having the same effect on the person questioned as when the inquisitor in an old espionage movie has a bright light shining in the captive's eyes: Don was to be seen only in harsh, threatening silhouette. The light from the window also bounced off the polished mahogany into our eyes. Bill sat next to Don, trying to appear nonchalant. I seated Carol next to the reporter across from Don, then politely asked Don if it would be OK for me to close the drapes to make it easier for Carol to see. Of course, I asked this as I was already reaching for the drapery pull. With the room now comfortably lit and the beverages served, the court reporter had Carol swear to tell the truth, the whole truth, and nothing but the truth.

Don went through the preliminaries: name, age, address, education, employment history. Then he started on the harder questions.

"So," he began, "tell us why you aren't working now."

She managed to show the same steel she'd had when Rosa had interviewed her. "Bill broke my neck and I'm still healing!" She glared at Don, meeting his gaze fully.

"Let's break that down. You claim that Bill broke your neck. How did that happen?"

"He came home drunk, got naked, while trying to rape me he put me in a full-Nelson hold, pushing my head forward until two vertebrae were crushed!"

"How did you get away?" Don appeared nonplussed by that stark statement. My stomach wrenched again as it always did when I heard Carol's trembling voice.

"I told him that I had to pee and get some lube."

"So...he just let you go?" Don said this with something between a sneer and a face showing disbelief. I knew his tone would change if he had the chance to read it back in court.

"Yes."

"He just released you and let you go." His tone was still disbelief.

"Yes."

"Did he say anything—anything at all?"

"No."

"OK, what did you do then?"

"I got out of the bed and walked toward the bathroom. Then I ran out the front door and across the street to Jill's house."

Don marinated his disbelief with sarcasm as he asked, "How were you able to run if your neck was broken?"

"I didn't know then that it was broken. And I didn't believe I'd have another chance to get away."

"What did you think had happened?"

"I'd heard a crunching sound and my neck hurt. I wasn't sure yet what had actually happened—only that it was bad."

"OK, what did you do next?"

"I rang the bell and pounded on their door. After a little while Jill opened the door, saw it was me, and told me to come in out of the cold." Carol was doing a good job of only answering the questions and not volunteering too much.

"What happened next?"

"Bill came out of our house yelling for me to get back there 'right now' as if I were a toddler."

"And then?"

"Jill told him 'Go to hell,' slammed the door, bolted it and rushed to the phone to call the police." Carol was starting to shake as she related this last part, as if reliving the terror.

"What happened next?"

"Jill grabbed a blanket from their couch and put it around me. Bill came to the door and started pounding. We told him we'd called the police and they were on their way."

"What were you wearing when you got to Jill's?"

"Nothing. I hadn't stopped for a robe or slippers."

"Why not?"

"I was afraid for my life."

"But you say that Bill had let you go. Why were you afraid?"

"I knew that if I'd stayed or gone back, Bill would have finished raping me without a care in the world."

"How could you possibly know that?"

"He'd raped me before."

"When was that?"

"Many times."

"Starting when?"

"On our honeymoon," she said.

Don looked at his yellow pad, then asked, "If he just let you go in February, had you ever before asked him to stop?"

"Yes."

"When?"

"Whenever he was hurting me."

"Did he ever stop when you said he was hurting you?"

"No."

"What would he do when you asked him to stop?"

"Most times, he'd just ignore me."

"And at other times?"

"He just said, 'shut up and enjoy it!'"

"Did you ever have sex when he didn't hurt you?" Don asked.

"Yes."

"What was different?"

"Sometimes he was tender and took his time."

"Back to the honeymoon. Were you hurt in any way?"

"Yes."

"How?"

"My vagina, my hips, my arms were all bruised and sore."

"Did you report it to any authorities?"

"No." Her head drooped, and she no longer met Don's eyes. I couldn't tell if it was from exhaustion or shame.

"Did you go to a doctor or hospital?" Don's tone was as caring as I'd ever heard him. Even if, to me, it was a put on.

"No," she said, quietly.

"Why not?"

"I was frightened, tired, and told myself there was nothing anybody could do about it."

"So we only have your word that this event even happened?"

"Bill knows."

"So it is just your word against his?" Don reverted to his sarcastic voice.

"If you put it that way, yes. But he knows." She looked at Bill with, what was for her, a hard stare.

"If what you are saying is true, why didn't you leave him then?"

"I was very tired. I was pregnant. We were at Disneyland. I didn't think, as his wife, that I had any choice."

"Anything else?"

Carol caught her breath. She raised her voice to a near shout. "I was pregnant and alone. I was frightened. I had no money of my own. I had nowhere to go and no way to get there!" She broke into sobs.

Don just sat there looking at her. Bill had a smile on his face, not a big grin, but that small, confident smile of every bully I'd ever met. I put my hand on Carol's shoulder and called for a break. I would have stopped the proceeding altogether, but I knew that Carol would have to testify to these same questions in court and she was doing as well as could be expected.

As we got up, Don said in a tone I could only describe as smarmy, "Let's take 10. But remember you won't be able to start Bill until I finish with Carol." I think he put undue emphasis on "finish," but I just replied, "I know." And we walked out.

Carol went into the bathroom, muttering she needed to wash her face and pull herself together. Still looking tired, she soon joined me in the hall. "I'm sorry," she said. "I just couldn't stand any more of the way he was asking those questions. What a scumbag!"

"Carol," I said, "unfortunately, all of this will be part of our case at some time or another. He has a right to ask the questions. His tone is disgusting, but it won't sound that way if or when he reads the transcript in court. I think you're doing a great job. Remember that he'll go through every incident you can remember and try to pin you down as much as possible on your ability to recall. You've gone over these events with Diane and you need to hang in there. OK?"

"What if I just refuse to answer any more?"

"That will mean that you couldn't tell a court about them later. We think you will have to talk about the other incidents of abuse. The effect they had on you impacts your ability to work.

If you are ever going to get damages in a personal injury case, you will have to be able to talk about them in open court."

She wasn't excited about it, but agreed to answer whatever was asked, unless I objected.

We went back into the conference room. Don and Bill were already seated, laughing about something. The court reporter sat back down with a blank look on her face and placed her hands over the keys on the reporting machine.

"Back on the record," Don said. "Will the court reporter please read back the last question and answer?"

When she had finished, Don asked, "Is there anything you want to add to your last answer?"

"I don't think so—right now," Carol said quietly.

Don seized on her answer. "You'll have the chance to review this deposition transcript before it becomes final. But if you don't make your additions and corrections promptly, you understand that you may never have the chance?"

"I think so," she said, her voice still low.

"Then let's move on. When was the next time you claim Bill forced himself upon you?"

Carol appeared to think for a moment. "I'm not sure, exactly, but it was a few months after Joey was born."

"What happened?"

"I think it was September or October of 1983. Another Saturday night. Bill went out drinking with some of his buddies and when he came home, he raped me."

"Did you ask him to stop?'

"Yes. I yelled at him to stop. But he wouldn't. He said it was his right as my husband to have sex with me whenever he wanted to."

"Did you seek medical attention or report this event to anybody?"

"No." Her answer was quiet, again.

"Why not? After all, you were not away from home, you had people you knew around you, but you didn't report it?"

I objected. "Don, that is compound, complex, and assumes facts not in evidence."

"Are you instructing the witness not to answer?"

"No, I'm just stating an objection for the record."

Don turned back to Carol and said, "You can answer the question."

She looked at me.

"You can answer the question if you understand it," I said.

Carol hesitated a few seconds. "I still had nowhere else to go and I was ashamed."

"Did you ever, at any time, go to a doctor for any of the times you allege Bill raped you?" Don pressed.

"Not until the last one." Her voice dropped to barely above a whisper.

"Do you claim that Bill ever hurt you in any other way, physically?"

"Yes. Many times."

"Did you ever seek medical treatment for any of these alleged injuries?"

"Yes."

"What injuries did you report?"

"A broken bone in my hand."

"How do you claim that Bill broke a bone in your hand?"

"He slammed a car door on it."

"Where did you go for treatment?"

"County Hospital."

"On Moorpark and Bascom?"

She paused, as if retracing her steps. "Yes."

"What did you tell them about your broken hand?"

"That it got slammed in a door."

"Did you tell them who had slammed the door on your hand?"

"Yes. Bill."

"Did you tell them that Bill had intentionally slammed a door on your hand?"

"No."

"What did you say?"

"That Bill had accidentally slammed the door on my hand."

"How do you know that isn't what actually happened?"

"By the look on his face when he did it."

"What is that supposed to mean?"

"He gave me that smug little smile—like he's wearing now—and walked away." We all looked at Bill who had switched to what could have been a look of concern on his face. I thought of a cat with a canary feather in the corner of its mouth.

"But you didn't report it as an intentional act on his part?"

"No."

"Why not?"

"Um, there were a couple of reasons. I wasn't sure what our insurance would cover. But mostly I was afraid of what he would do to me next if I had reported him."

"What did you think he might do?"

"More punching me in the ribs, screaming at me, scaring Joey, I don't know what else."

"Did you ever report any of these types of behavior to any authorities or medical professionals?"

"No."

"Did you ever tell anyone?"

"Not until after the last one."

"When you *claim* he broke your neck in February?" I would have objected to the overly sarcastic way he emphasized her choice of the word, but knew that would only make me sound whiney when it was read back.

After a beat, Carol replied, "Yes. But it is not just a claim. It is the truth."

Don jotted some notes. "Who did you tell?"

I jumped in to clarify. "Other than your lawyer."

Carol nodded. "My friend Jill and my therapist. And Dr. Anton."

"What did you tell them?" Don asked.

"The same things I've told you."

Don changed the line of his questions delving into the details of their custody arrangement, then switched back. "So tell me why you say you cannot work."

Carol paused. We had rehearsed this answer. "My doctors tell me that the bones in my neck are just about healed, but not the muscles and ligaments. I still have a 15-pound lifting limit and they don't want me turning my head around much. When I do, I get headaches, real bad ones. Then I have to take a special medication that makes me sleepy."

Don looked at his notes then back at Carol. "So you are saying that you can't work because you get sleepy?"

I put my hand on Carol's arm to stop her. "Counsel, that is a complete mischaracterization of her answer. Carol, don't answer the question."

"So you won't let the witness answer the question?" Don put on his best bluster.

"I won't let her respond to questions that can be read back to mischaracterize her testimony. Now, if you want to ask her whether her prescribed medications—for the headaches secondary to her injuries—make her too sleepy to work, go ahead. But that has been asked and answered."

Don gave me a grin and turned back to Carol. "What were your duties when you were working at the gas station?"

Carol ran down the list: time as a cashier; moving boxes of lighters, cigarettes, snacks, automotive oil, anti-freeze, windshield-washing fluid, and other small automotive products; putting the products on shelves in the small area where the cash register was.

"By snacks, you mean small bags of potato chips, pretzels, nuts?" Don asked.

Carol processed the question for a moment. "In part. But I would have to go to the storage room where the boxes of those snacks were stacked. Sometimes I'd have to get on a ladder to reach what we needed. Then I'd have to carry them into the cashier area, unbox the bags, then insert them into the clips on the stands where the customers would see them at eye level. There was a lot of balancing to be done while re-stocking. And while the snacks were relatively light, the fluids weighed a lot. There was a lot of bending over and twisting involved."

Don frowned, obviously unhappy she hadn't fallen into a trap. Good girl, I thought.

"Well, that was non-responsive!" Don remarked. "Weren't there other employees that could have done the lifting and transport of these snacks?"

"Of course there were other employees, but they were working on cars. Our owner would have been pissed if they were taking time away from their other duties to help me. I hope he'll even hire me back when I'm cleared by the doctors."

"Could you find a job where you wouldn't have those extra duties?"

"I've been looking at the ads in the newspaper, but haven't seen anything that I'm qualified for. But I'll start making applications as soon as I'm cleared by the doctors." Carol knew she was doing OK and gave me a little smile.

I leaned over and whispered confirmation in her ear. "You are doing fine."

Don asked, "Have the doctors told you when you should be able to go back to work?"

"I'm hoping sometime in the next couple of months, but that depends on how well I continue to heal."

"How much were you making at the gas station?" Don had her paystubs as part of the disclosure packages we'd exchanged, but asked anyway.

"It was pretty much minimum wage. You have the paycheck, but I think about $3.50 an hour."

"And what do the jobs you are looking at now pay?"

"I'm not sure, because I haven't actually applied yet. But probably about the same $3.50-4.00 an hour."

"So, that would be about $160 per week?"

"I haven't done the math. Is that for a 40-hour week?"

"Yes," Don said. "40 hours at $4.00 is $160."

"If I could, I'd take that job. I never got 40 hours in a week at the gas station. The most I ever got was 30 or 35."

"Did you get tips?"

"Sometimes people would put pennies or nickels from their change into the tip jar, but I never came home with more than a few dollars."

"Have you considered getting training that could land you a higher-paying job?"

"I'd like to, but I'd have to be able to study and still support myself somehow."

"Aren't you living with your parents?"

"Yes. Me and Joey stay with my mom and dad at their house until I'm well enough to leave."

"Could you stay there and go to school?"

"I appreciate my folks and all, but we don't get along that great since I married Bill."

"Can you say why?"

"Mom is all, 'I told you so!' all the time. She always said she thought something was just wrong with Bill. And we're not all on the same page about how to raise Joey."

I asked Don how much longer he meant to go. There wasn't an important topic he hadn't covered, so continuing would have just been to annoy us. He surprised me by saying he was done for the time being and we could start Bill's deposition at 1:30.

* * * * *

"Why would Don stop and not get a whole list of the incidents?" Harris asked.

"It didn't matter to him," I responded. "He had made his point that it was always going to be her word against Bill's and that she would never have corroboration. So, to Don, it would be no different if it were twice more or twenty."

"And you were OK with that?"

"Yes. Because I knew that Dr. Gold would be able to testify to all the times Carol had told her about, and explain why, in each case, Carol would not have gone to the police—or even tell her parents. Not even Jill! She was too ashamed and simply didn't even have the words to express herself to describe her situation."

"I guess it takes a lot of guts for the victim to step forward," Harris commented, wearing a troubled expression.

"Back then more than now, I hope. But even with a different culture today, there are all sorts of victims who hesitate for a variety of reasons. This case opened my eyes to the reality of what can and does happen behind closed doors." I took a deep breath to resettle my emotions. "But there's more."

36 - Bill's Deposition

June 10, 1985

The day had warmed up. I took Carol over to a deli in the Pruneyard plaza across from Don's office. It was nice enough to eat under the large overhang outside the deli. Carol was quite relieved to be done with her deposition but really didn't want to stay for Bill's. While he had given her a hard stare for much of the time that she was detailing his physical abuse, he had still been better behaved than I'd expected. I knew we'd find out more about his self-control as we got into his deposition. I told her it was important that she stay with me for Bill's deposition because she was going to have to give me feedback on his answers and maybe suggest follow-up questions.

Back in Don's office, with a fresh cup of coffee, Bill and I were across the table from each other next to the same court reporter.

I had the reporter swear Bill in, then began with the same basic questions as Don had used as preliminaries. I was surprised by some of the answers.

"Where are you working?"

"I'm still not working!"

"You're not working?"

"Nope. Got fired!"

"Weren't you working for your father's construction company?"

"Yes."

"What were you doing there?"

"Whatever he told me."

"Can you be more specific?"

"Sometimes he'd have me doing general labor on a site, sometimes I'd be doing punch list duty to sign off on a completed project. Maybe drive a tractor."

"What do 'general labor' duties entail?"

"General labor could be anything from moving a pile of crap from one side of a yard to the other. Or I could be digging a hole. Or nailing framing for a concrete pour. General stuff."

"Who decided what you were doing?"

"Either my dad or one of the foremen."

"You didn't have a supervisory position?"

"Nope."

"Why not?"

"Dad wanted me to spend more time at the bottom of the dung heap. Said it would make me a better contractor in the end."

"Were you studying to be a contractor?"

"I wish—no, I don't. Too much math."

"So why were you fired?"

"He said none of the foremen liked my attitude."

"Did you ever drive the heavy equipment?"

"Yes. I told you I'd sometimes drive a tractor."

"Did that pay differently from general labor?"

"Yes, for the other guys at the sites. But not for me. I was labeled as general labor as a job description."

I made a note to have Jules, our investigator, check out some job sites and foremen.

I continued that line of questioning. "Are you looking for work?" June was a time for full employment in the construction trades and I knew that if you could breathe, jokingly referred to as fogging a mirror, you could find a job if you wanted one.

"I called around, but nobody I knew was hiring."

"So where are you getting the money to live on?" In his Income and Expense Declaration, Bill had listed monthly expenses of almost $2,500.

"I'm borrowing from my folks. I think I owe them about $10,000, so far."

"Are you signing promissory notes to them?"

"What's that?"

I knew he was playing with me, but needed to tie him down. "Written IOUs."

"Nah. Dad says he's keeping a ledger or something."

"Has he put a limit on how much longer he is going to support you like this?"

"I guess until I piss him off enough that he stops. So far so good, though."

I'd seen this scam before. "So rather than even have you digging holes, he's just loaning you money so you don't have to work."

The smug bastard just smiled. "Yup!"

This was consistent with what Don had said at our last meeting with Judge DePalma. So I asked, "Have you talked to him about borrowing the money to pay the support and attorney fees that were just ordered?"

He looked at Don, who just nodded. Bill said, "Yes. He has agreed to front me that money, too."

"Are you still living at the house on Vistamont?"

"Nope."

"What happened to that house?"

"Had to sign it over to my Dad." That smug smile again.

"Why?"

"He'd put up the money for the down payment. Then, when I got fired, he demanded that I sign it over to him or he wouldn't loan me any money."

"Where are you living? Your Disclosure documents said Vistamont."

"I'm living with my girlfriend."

"What is her name?"

Don objected. "Her name is not relevant or material to this proceeding and I'm instructing him not to answer."

I looked at him with surprise. "I guess we'll have to talk to a judge about that. But let's move on. Mr. Collins, what is your current address?"

"Same objection!" Don said. "Don't answer that." He turned from Bill to me. "Just use his parents' house." Don gave me their address in Saratoga.

"I guess that will give the judge two things to decide. But could you tell me how where he lives, and with whom, wouldn't be relevant to our spousal support, child support, and visitation issues?"

Don didn't budge. "I guess we'll find out."

"OK, Mr. Collins, are you sharing any expenses with your girlfriend?"

"Nope. But I do some chores, like fixing the plumbing. Stuff like that."

I was starting to think my investigation bill was going to get blown up as big as a balloon. I was certainly curious about where he'd find a woman to let him freeload at her place like that.

I shifted gears. "I'd like to direct your attention to the night of February 9, 1985. Do you remember that?"

"Is that the night Carol said I raped her?"

"Yes. Do you remember it?"

"Sorta. I was pretty drunk when I got home."

"Do you remember Carol being asleep when you got home?"

"Not really. I got into bed and she kinda looked at me over her shoulder then rolled back away from me."

"What happened next?"

"I asked her if she felt like playing around."

"What did she say?"

"She didn't say anything."

"What did she do?"

"She kinda stuck her naked butt at me. I took that as a yes and got started."

"What do you mean by got started? Did you put her in some kind of wrestling hold?"

"Yeah. I put my arms around her shoulders and my hands on her head, like she said. But I never pushed down or tried to hurt her. It was just the kind of stuff we did as part of having sex. Kinda like foreplay, I think you call it."

"What happened next?"

"She said she had to pee and wanted some lube or something, so I let her go and she ran out of the house."

"When you said you let her get up, what did you mean by that?"

"Well, I let her loose from my arms like she asked."

"Did she tell you she was hurt?"

"No. Just that she needed to go to the bathroom."

"Did she ever tell you to stop—that you were hurting her?"

"No." He shook his head.

"Did she do or say anything about being in pain?"

"No."

"Did she cry?"

"No."

"What did you do when she ran out of the house?"

"I put on my pants and went after her."

"Did you see where she'd gone?"

"Yeah. Jill's."

"Did you follow her there?"

"Yeah. I went there to find out what was wrong."

I hoped to trip him up a bit. "When we were just starting the divorce proceedings, didn't you say something about Carol's broken neck having been caused by her tripping on something or other?"

Bill looked at Carol, then back at me. He leaned toward me and smiled. "I never said anything like that. It was always, you know, about how she liked to have sex. I don't know where you could have heard that stuff." His smile grew even broader. Don's attention remained fixated on the papers in front of him, appearing as if he wanted to bury his head in them, too.

I took a deep, settling breath. "When you got to Jill's, did you make a lot of noise banging on the door?"

"Well, I saw her go inside, so I went to the door and knocked. They didn't answer. So I guess I did bang on it. It was frustrating, you know, that I knew they were there but wouldn't answer the door. Then they shouted something about the police, so I went home."

"Did the police come to your house that night?"

"Yeah. About 3:30."

"What happened?"

"They arrested me, took me to jail."

"How long did they keep you there?"

"I don't remember, exactly. I remember being booked, calling my Dad, and being let go a little later with a promise to show up for a court date."

"For the April 7th preliminary hearing?"

"Yeah, that one."

I looked at Don. "Do you know what the status is in the criminal proceeding?"

Don held his hand up to stop Bill from answering. "You'll have to check with the court or Robert Paladino," Don said. "He's handling the criminal proceeding. I don't have any information since the continuance. And I'm not going to let you ask any more questions that relate to the criminal charges until those are resolved."

"Have you ever sexually forced yourself on Carol?" I wanted to push him to invoke the Fifth Amendment to create that aura of guilt.

As expected, Bill did, reading from a sheet in front of him. "On the advice of my attorney I'm not going to answer that question and I invoke my rights under the Fifth Amendment to the Constitution of the United States," he intoned.

With that statement on the record, it was clear I wasn't going to get any real answers until a judge ordered them, so we wrapped it up.

37 - Custody Hearing & Special Master

June 12, 1985

Kathryn Monahan was already in the courtroom with her evaluation when Carol and I showed up at 9 o'clock that morning. I didn't see either Don or Bill. I checked in with Judge DePalma's clerk as required by protocol, and she informed me that Don had called to tell her he would be delayed; he was appearing in another department. So I took the opportunity to have Kathryn give me a preview of her recommendations. She reaffirmed that she believed Carol as to the rape and other abuse, but was still recommending a joint child sharing schedule.

"Here's the deal, Steve," Kathryn said. "Even if I think Bill is not a nice person, together with the support he receives from his parents and his physical condition, I believe he can actually parent as well as Carol. She is too fragile both emotionally and physically. She is still having trouble taking care of herself."

"What do you mean by 'too fragile'?" I asked.

"Do you remember having a toddler? They require constant supervision to keep them from killing themselves. They throw tantrums that challenge even healthy parents. Carol doesn't yet have the physical stamina and strength, let alone the emotional strength, to deal with Joey for more time than she's getting, even with help from her parents and Jill. The pressure of a toddler is full time and could leave Carol locked in her room, frozen with doubt and insecurity. This could lead to harm to Joey or even to Carol, herself."

"How likely is it that Carol would hurt herself or Joey?"

Kathryn shook her head. "Who knows, for sure? Maybe Dr. Gold could give you a better answer."

"Have you talked with the grandparents?"

"Yes," she said. "As you'll read in my report, I've spoken to them all by phone. I liked Arnold, Carol's dad, the best. He is calm and supportive. Arlene adds stressors, as does Thomas, Bill's dad. Bill's mom, Mary, is closest to Arnold in going with the flow. There was nothing from any of them that would get in the way of the child sharing arrangement we've worked out."

"OK," I said, trying to hide my disappointment. "Have you checked where Bill will be living with Joey? Have you talked with his girlfriend?"

"Whoa," she said. "That is news to me. I didn't know he wasn't living in the Vistamont house. That's what he'd told me. He also said he was going to leave Joey with his parents while he was at work."

"In his deposition, two days ago, he said he had been fired, was not now working, and was living with his girlfriend. Don wouldn't let him answer about his girlfriend's name or address."

Dismay crossed Kathryn's face. "Well, when we see the judge, I'll have to ask for the opportunity to do a supplemental report. But please understand that I still don't think Carol is capable of sole custody."

I was sanguine. "How long do you think you'll need?"

"Maybe a couple of weeks, depending on the level of cooperation."

At 9:30 a.m. Don showed up with Bill. A few minutes later we were all sitting in Judge DePalma's chambers. Don apologized to the judge and Kathryn explained to Judge DePalma what she'd already told me. Then she informed the judge that she'd just learned that Bill's living situation was not what appeared to be in her report, and that she'd like to meet with the girlfriend to better understand the impact she would be having on Joey.

I followed up immediately, and asked the judge to allow us to depose the girlfriend, explaining that, at Bill's deposition two days ago, Don had not allowed us to even know her name, and now we find out she will be de facto co-parenting the child.

The judge looked at Don with one eyebrow arched.

Taking the signal, Don said, "We don't want her harassed by Mr. Gregory. If she were to be interviewed by Ms. Monahan and it looked like she'd need to be a witness, we'd concede the need for her to be deposed. But for now, we think Ms. Monahan should be able to ask the necessary questions of the girlfriend."

Seeing me about to jump out of my seat, Judge DePalma held up his palm to me to stay silent. "Mr. Gregory, I understand your concerns. I trust Ms. Monahan to investigate the living situation and report back to us all. How much time do you need, Ms. Monahan?"

Before Kathryn could answer, Don spoke up. "Bill's girlfriend has a 9-to-5 job during the week. It would be a hardship on her to have to take off work to come downtown to meet with Ms. Monahan. Is there a way this could be done over the phone or at night, or on the weekend?"

I broke in before Kathryn could respond. "How can you get a real sense of the girlfriend without seeing her in her own living environment?"

Kathryn flashed an understanding smile at us. "Unfortunately, this is a common problem in Family Court. We do have to rely on phone interviews all too often, like we did with the grandparents. While they may not be perfect, I think we could start over the phone and then go from there."

The judge supported her recommendation. Bill would tell the girlfriend that Kathryn would call and then they would decide whether an in-person interview was necessary. Pending further hearings and information, the temporary sharing arrangement would stay in place. That meant that Joey, who had just turned two years old, would still be moving from one grandparents' house to the others' every three to four days.

Informing the judge about the other problems we'd had with testimony at the depositions, I asked him to appoint a special master, someone tasked to make evidentiary rulings on the spot. If one side disagreed with the master's ruling, they could stop and demand a judge rule, but would then be subject to serious financial penalties if wrong.

Judge DePalma turned to Don. "Do you have any problems with my appointing a discovery master, Mr. Fraser?" His tone suggested he would do so whether or not Don agreed. Wisely, Don said he'd be OK with that if we shared the cost equally. I couldn't refuse. The judge appointed Linda Porter, someone I didn't know.

But back at the office, both Marty and Sue were excited by the news of Linda Porter as special discovery master. Marty said she'd held the same position in one of his cases and we couldn't have asked for a better master. Not that she was biased, but she knew her rules of evidence and had experience with domestic violence when she had been a DA.

38 - Monahan Reports on Bill's Girlfriend

June 19, 1985

After a week had passed and I hadn't heard anything, I called Kathryn Monahan's office to leave a message. She called back about a half hour later.

"What's up?" Kathryn asked.

"That's what I want to know. Have you heard from Bill Collins' girlfriend?"

"Actually, I was able to reach her this morning."

"And?"

"Nothing much. Apparently, during most of Bill's time with Joey, the girlfriend is at work. She hasn't spent much time with Joey since Joey likes to spend the night with Bill's parents who have quite a set-up for him."

"Did you learn anything?"

"She seemed really attached to Joey, despite not having had much time with him. She says she had done a lot of babysitting as a teenager and that Joey is well-behaved for a boy who isn't even three yet. She volunteered that Bill really gets involved with Joey and that Joey loves to play with Bill."

"If she is at work and Bill is not working, why is Joey spending so much time at Thomas and Mary's house?" I asked. "Why isn't Bill watching Joey?"

"Michelle, the girlfriend, thinks that Bill does his watching at his parent's house. They are more set up for the toddler.

Apparently, Joey is having trouble with his potty training and I don't think Bill likes changing diapers."

"Do we know her full name? Where she works? Where they live?"

"Her name is Michelle Barnes. She works at a Togo's on Story Road in San Jose and they live in a rental apartment on McKinley street near Costco." She gave me the address.

"Did you ask about her relationship with Bill? Are they planning on marrying when the divorce is over? I'd love to know how he treats her. Does she have any family in the area?"

Kathryn chuckled. "Slow down. You may get a chance to ask her those questions in person. Since she is a significant person in Joey's life, I'm going to report that there is a lot we don't know—including the questions you are asking."

39 - Criminal Update

July 8, 1985

In the almost four weeks since I'd talked with Kathryn, I'd been working hard on other cases that actually helped me pay the overhead. But on Monday, July 8, as I sat with Marty, Sue and Jules planning our week, Jules got a message from his contact at the DA's office.

They had cut a deal with Bill last Friday, July 5.

He had pled no contest to a misdemeanor charge of domestic battery and had accepted a sentence of three months to be followed by two years of probation. The deal had been cut and executed without notice to Carol or our office. Even odder, there was not even a sentencing report from the Adult Probation Department. Bill was given six months to get his affairs in order before serving his sentence which would begin Dec 28, 1985.

I was blown away by the terrible news. Dumbfounded, I just vented aloud. "How the hell does that even happen? No public notice, no felony...not even a sentencing report! It just doesn't make sense!"

Even Marty, the sage, unflappable Marty, had to stand up and walk around. After sputtering a moment under his breath, he said, "Why don't you call Plato, Steve? Then we'll go for a run."

I went back to my office and placed the call. Amazingly, Plato took my call. Keeping my temper in check, I asked him about the deal for Bill, and was shocked at his answer: he said he didn't know and hadn't had anything to do with the case since the preliminary in March when he was about to add additional charges. He had no idea how the deal could have happened. Since he'd been taken off the case, he didn't know who was in charge of it. He promised to check and get back to me later that day.

Our run that day was faster than usual. After whining for the first half mile, we stayed in our own heads and stepped up the pace. We couldn't talk; we had to concentrate on keeping our arms loose and just breathing. It didn't solve anything, but we both felt better when we got back to the Y.

Plato called back just after 4:15 p.m. He explained that the DA in charge of the Sexual Crimes Division, Paul Taglio, himself had signed off on the deal. It was approved by Judge Stanley. He had no explanation as to why we hadn't been informed and why there was no sentencing report. Or even why there was a six-month gap before Bill would start serving a three-month sentence. We speculated it might have something to do with the practice of certain sentences being commuted during the break between Christmas and New Year's in a kind of spirit-of-the-season goodwill gesture. In any event, it was clear there was nothing else he could do but wish us well. His tone told me that he found this almost as distasteful as I did, adding, "Somehow the system failed her. I wish I could tell you how it happened."

I also asked him if he had found out anything about the restraining order. He said it had been removed, effective today. I thanked him and relayed the information to the team, then called Carol to let her know we would apply for a Family Court Restraining Order.

* * * * *

Harris had grown agitated at this latest piece of bad news. "That sounds like corruption even to me! So he barely gets his wrist slapped for breaking his wife's neck? How is that justice?"

"Remember," I said, "there are a few things in play: the press had no inkling of what had happened with the plea or sentencing. And this is a story about Carol. Bill is a different story, for another time."

Mollified, Harris made a circular motion with his right hand, so I continued.

40 - Personal Injury Case & Restraining Order

July 12-15, 1985

After hearing the latest news from Plato, Marty was as angry as I was. Neither of us cooled down much over the next few days, so we decided to go ahead with the personal injury case, which he would draft and file.

Marty managed to get the paperwork done by the following Monday, July 15. At the same time, I'd prepared the application for a Family Court Restraining Order. We had Jules walk them both through the court and serve them on Bill that night, along with a subpoena for Michelle Barnes to appear for her deposition on August 28.

Guessing correctly that he'd find them at Michelle's apartment, while serving the subpoena Jules took a quick glance around at their living situation. He reported that it looked like a typical one-bedroom unit on the second floor of a working-class neighborhood apartment house: four stories, a small pool in the center of a courtyard, plenty of cement, cars parked behind the building in assigned spaces with small storage areas on the walls of the carport. Jules even asked a few of the other apartment dwellers if there had been any sounds of disruption or fighting coming from that apartment. One of the neighbors said they'd heard some shouting that seemed directed at a child that was sometimes there, but other than that Jules could not turn up anything.

I got a call from Don the next morning. He had received our application for a Restraining Order.

"I didn't know anything about the plea or the pulling of the R.O.," Don said. "We'll stipulate to your request. I'm sure DePalma would grant it anyway. OK?"

Relieved, I agreed. We made arrangements for the paperwork and he promised an Answer to the Complaint within the 30 days.

41 - Michelle Barnes' Deposition

Linda Porter was perfect for our discovery issues: a short Black woman with an intensity that would tolerate no nonsense. She had close-cropped hair and wore a stylish business pantsuit, John-Lennon-type glasses, no lipstick. Through the grapevine, Marty had learned she worked in the DA's office for almost 10 years before deciding she would have to get out before she completely lost her faith in humanity. While with the DA, she worked her way up from misdemeanor arraignments to felony trials, including cases involving drug-related crimes and domestic violence.

In preparation for this round of depositions, Linda had spoken to Don and me on a conference call and, after listening to our complaints and bickering, quickly disabused us of any more nonsense. I would get to question Michelle Barnes at 9:30 a.m. I told them I'd subpoenaed Thomas Collins for 10:30 a.m. I also wanted to finish my deposition of Bill, and then Don would get a chance to follow up with Carol that afternoon. Because the criminal case was now decided, for better or worse, I'd at least get to question Bill about past behavior. I told Linda what I'd heard about Bill's sentence, the lack of notice to the victim, and the removal of the restraining order. She was as surprised as I'd been, but said that wasn't part of her assignment.

The depositions were at my downtown offices. The view that day was less magnificent than usual. The eastern foothills were still tan, but the morning sky had a hint of smoke from a nearby fire. The day promised to be hot, in more ways than one.

Reluctantly, I pulled the drapes before Don had to ask. We started promptly.

My initial impression of Michelle was that she and Carol could have been sisters. Both were about the same height, with long dark hair, hazel eyes and late 20s. She came clad in what looked like some of her best clothes, perhaps knowing Carol would be there: a demure navy dress with a thin gold chain dangling a tiny diamond pendant, nylons, and low heels.

After she was sworn in by the court reporter, I had her give us her full name, address, and other particulars. She told us she worked at a Togo's on Story Road; she'd been there about six months; she had graduated from Willow Glen High School in 1976 and was taking classes at San Jose City Junior College with a view toward transferring to San Jose State for the fall semester in 1987. She planned to major in business. It all sounded eerily familiar.

I asked, "Does anyone else live in your apartment with you?"

"Yes, Bill and Joey."

"How long have they lived there with you?"

"Since June of this year."

"So that is two or two and a half months?"

"Roughly."

"Do you have a financial arrangement with Bill?"

"Yes."

"What is that financial arrangement?" Clearly she was following instructions on only answering the question that was asked.

"He will be responsible for paying half of the rent and expenses, including utilities and food."

"Has he paid you anything for June, July, or August?"

"No."

"Has he given you money for anything since he moved in?"

"No."

"Not even food?"

"No."

"Do you keep track of those expenses in a journal of any kind?"

"Yes."

"Did you bring it with you today?"

"No."

"Will you supply it without the necessity of a subpoena?"

She looked at Don who shook his head. "No," Michelle said.

I turned to Linda Porter. She said, "Mr. Fraser, it appears you have a relationship with this witness. Why don't you agree to produce it within a week?"

Don looked back to Michelle and raised his eyebrows in a questioning way.

"OK," Michelle said. "I'll give a copy to Mr. Fraser."

"And Mr. Fraser," Linda followed up, "you'll have it to Mr. Gregory by Tuesday, September 10th?"

Don agreed to that timeline.

I continued my questioning. "Ms. Barnes, do you have an agreement as to when Bill Collins will be required to repay the amounts being logged in this journal?"

"Yes." Back to one-word answers.

"When would that be?"

"He promised to start making payments as soon as he has a paycheck again."

"Do you know what efforts he is making to return to work?"

"Only what he has told me."

"What has he told you?"

"That nobody is hiring right now. That the busy season for construction is over."

"So, to the best of your knowledge, it is now the end of August 1985, and he is not looking for any kind of construction job at the present time?"

"I think that is what I said!"

"I was just clarifying. When did you meet Bill?"

"We've known each other for years. Maybe late '70s? I'm not sure."

"When did you start dating?"

"Sometime in the late '70s or early '80s."

"So, to be clear, you had dated Bill before he married Carol?"

"Yes."

"When did you break up?"

"Sometime in the summer of 1982."

"About when he started dating Carol?"

"That seems about right." She glanced at Carol. It wasn't friendly.

I decided it was time to switch gears. "How do things work with Joey?"

"What do you mean?"

"Do you get along with him?"

"Yes. He is a wonderful little boy!" A smile lit her face.

"What do you mean by 'wonderful'?"

"He's happy most of the time, he tries to please, and he's always ready to play a game."

"What kind of game?"

"He loves to pile blocks, then knocks them down and claps his hands. He squeals to play chase, and he'll even make a game of putting his toys away in the box we have in the living area."

"How many bedrooms does your apartment have?"

"One."

"Bathrooms?"

"One."

"Where does Joey sleep?"

"There is a crib in a corner of the living area. We start him in the big bed and then move him to the crib when we go to bed at night."

"Do you and Bill have sex when Joey is in his crib?"

"That is none of your damn business!" Bill shouted.

Don put a hand on Bill's arm. "Steve...really. I object to the question as an invasion of privacy and not relevant to these proceedings."

Linda raised an eyebrow at me. "Mr. Gregory?"

"I believe it is relevant to both cases. What goes on in proximity to Joey is relevant to the child sharing and custody questions in the divorce case, and Bill's current behavior is relevant to the personal injury case to establish patterns of behavior."

Linda agreed with me and allowed us to go on, but not before Don had restated his objection, "For the record."

I had the court reporter read back the question.

"Yes," Michelle answered, "we have sex when Joey is staying with us."

"When did you first have sex with Bill?"

"I don't remember."

"Was it when you were dating before you broke up?"

"Yes."

"How long were you dating before you started having sex?"

"Four or five months, I think."

"So, you and Bill have had sexual relations in the late '70s, early '80s and now in the middle '80s?"

"Yes."

"More than 100 times in total?"

Michelle reddened, her eyes flashing in anger. Then she looked at Carol who was shrinking into her chair, her arms crossed, her head down. "Way more!" she exclaimed, as a smile crossed her lips, obviously not embarrassed.

"OK, during any of those 'way more' than 100 times you've had sex with Bill, has he ever hurt you?"

Don jerked forward in his seat. "Don't answer!" he shouted. "This is way beyond any rational relevancy. I object and ask that Mr. Gregory be admonished against further inquiry in this vein."

Linda stayed silent, and looked at me for a response.

I had prepared for this. "Whether Bill actually hurts partners is part and parcel of our claims for personal injury damages, and also bears on his fitness as a parent in custody proceedings. You have seen the pleadings and know we are seeking punitive damages as well as compensatory damages." My voice rose with each word, my emotions getting the better of me.

Linda put out a hand, palm facing me, to stop any further outburst. "I get it." She looked at Don. "I will allow the line of questioning and direct the witness to answer."

Michelle glanced at Don, who still was rigid with anger. Bill appeared ready to explode. Silence fell over the room for long seconds.

Linda spoke up and turned to Michelle. "Do you need to have the question repeated?"

"Yes, please," Michelle said.

"Has Bill ever hurt you physically while having sex?" I asked.

"Not really. I'm not sure what you mean."

"Have you ever sought medical attention as a result of something that happened while you and Bill were having sex?"

"Yes."

"Would you explain? No, wait, let me rephrase that. How many times have you sought medical attention as a result of something that happened while you and Bill were having sex?"

She thought for a while, then looked at Don, who shook his head and turned toward Linda Porter, an expression of disbelief on his face.

Porter simply met his gaze, and instructed, "You may answer the question."

"Twice," Michelle said. "I went to the doctor twice."

"When was the first time?"

"Sometime right before we broke up."

"What was the injury?"

"My shoulder."

"What happened to your shoulder?"

"The doctor said it was something in my rotator cuff."

"Did he ask how you hurt it?"

"Yes."

"What did you tell him?"

"That I hurt it lifting weights at the gym."

"What did Bill do to you that caused the injury?"

"He was pulling my arm behind my back."

"I'm trying to be delicate here. Was he in front of you or behind you?"

"Behind me."

"Had he done this to you before?"

"Yes, but not so rough."

"Did you ask him to stop?"

Don interrupted. "Objection. Vague. Which time?"

I looked back at Michelle. "The first time...the time we're talking about."

"Yes, I told him he was hurting me and he stopped."

"Did he hurt you again between that first time and the next time you had to go to the doctor?"

"Yes, but not badly."

I was surprised she'd offer that. "What do you mean by 'not badly'?"

"Maybe a muscle-pull or a bruise."

"Did you do anything for treatment?"

"Um, yes. Maybe some aspirin, an ice pack. It would go away after a few days."

I was intrigued. "And how often would these 'not badly' injuries happen?"

"Every three or four weeks."

Her response surprised me. "So this was part of your regular sex practice?" I clarified.

"Yes."

Walking the line, I asked, "Do you have a safe word to get him to stop?"

"Yes. Now we do. 'Halo.'" She gave Carol a sideways glance as she said it.

Shocked by the answer, I looked at Carol and caught her wince, saw her hand going to her neck. I couldn't react verbally—we were on the record.

I continued. "How many times have you used it?"

"Never." It seemed like she was on the verge of laughter.

"To clarify, you said Bill hurt your rotator cuff in the summer of 1982. Is that correct?"

"I think so."

"And the second time you needed to see a doctor was after you and Bill got back together?"

"Yes."

"When was that?"

"I think sometime this last spring."

"That would be March or April 1985?"

"Yes."

"Which doctor did you see?"

"Someone in the emergency room at Kaiser Hospital."

"The second time, the time you needed to see the doctor again, had you asked Bill to stop?"

"Yes, but after I was already hurt again."

"What did he do next?"

"He stopped and let go of my arm."

"Did he say or do anything else?"

"Well, he said 'Sorry' and we finished having sex."

"What time of day or night was that?"

"About two in the morning."

"Had you been together all evening?"

"No. He had been out with some of his friends."

"Were they drinking alcohol?"

"Yes."

"Before that time, had Bill ever hurt you when you weren't having sex?"

"A couple of times, we'd be arguing about something, you know, and he slapped me."

"Did he apologize?"

"Yes, he'd be very sweet, you know, and ask me to forgive him."

"I take it you did forgive him?"

"Yes."

"Did he do anything special to make up?"

She smiled a little. "He'd take me to a nice restaurant...with tablecloths."

"Did you get any treatment for your rotator cuff in 1982?"

"Yes. The doctor told me to take Motrin and, um, ice my shoulder with a special ice pack. And he put my arm in a sling."

"Anything else?"

"He gave me some exercises to do when it stopped hurting. And he said that if it didn't stop hurting within 10 days to come back and he'd give me a shot of some kind."

"Did you go back for the shot?"

"Yes. I hate needles, but my arm wasn't getting any better."

"Do you remember if the shot was cortisone?"

"Yeah, that's it."

"Did it help?"

"Yeah, after about an hour my shoulder stopped hurting."

"Did you do the exercises?"

"Yes."

"How is your shoulder now?"

"Fine."

"You said there was a second time Bill had hurt you during sex and you went to the doctor. When was that?"

"A couple of months ago. This spring, I think."

"What happened?"

"He twisted my wrist."

"Did you have X-rays taken?"

"Yes. I'd thought it was broken."

"Was it?"

"No. It was a sprain."

"Did you get some kind of brace?"

"Yeah. Something with plastic and Velcro, you know? I had to wear it for a week."

"Did you get another nice dinner?"

"Yeah. That nice restaurant in New Almaden."

"Was Joey staying with you when he hurt your wrist?"

"Yes."

"Did you wake him?"

"Yeah. I screamed and he woke up, you know, and started crying."

"Did you go to the doctor that night?"

"No, the next day."

"What time of night did you get hurt?"

"About two."

"And had Bill been out drinking with his friends, again?"

"Yes."

"What did you tell the doctor?"

"That I tripped and fell on my wrist."

"Did you go to the same doctor for both injuries?"

"No. I have Kaiser and I just went to the E.R., you know."

"Has Bill told you anything about his financial arrangements with his father?"

"Just that he has been borrowing money from him."

"But not enough to contribute to your living expenses?"

"I guess not, no. But enough to cover his car and insurance and stuff."

"After you and Bill got back together, has he said anything about what happened with the house on Vistamont?"

"Only that he had to sign it over to his dad."

"Did he say why?"

"No."

"How often does Bill go out drinking with his friends at night?"

"A couple of times a month."

"When you went to Kaiser for the second injury, what did you tell Joey?"

"That me and his daddy were playing and I accidently got hurt."

"How did Joey take that?"

"What do you mean?"

"What did Joey say or do when you told him that you and Bill were playing and you got hurt?"

"He moved his shoulders and said, 'Me too.'"

"Did you ask him what he meant by that?"

"No."

"Did you ask him what Daddy did that hurt him?"

"No."

"Did you ask him what was hurt?"

"No. He just pointed to his own wrist and I didn't want him to get upset with more questions."

It took all my willpower to keep my face blank and temper in check. I thanked Michelle for being there and said I had no further questions for her. Don declined to ask anything. Linda told Michelle that she was excused and could leave. We took a short break. During the break, Carol asked me tearfully whether the testimony of Michelle that Bill had hurt Joey would help her get custody. I said we could share that information with Kathryn, but without more, I didn't think it would make much of a difference.

42 - Thomas Collins' Deposition

August 28, 1985

Thomas Collins wore a navy suit, starched white shirt and a red-and-blue-striped tie, looking cool as a cucumber as he settled into his seat.

After the preliminaries, I asked him, "Have you ever had your deposition taken before today?"

"Yes," he replied. "Many times."

"Do you know how many?"

"Probably 15-20. It's not uncommon in the building industry. They say that no big job is over until the lawsuits have been settled."

"Have all those depositions been in connection with construction projects?"

"Yes."

"Have you met with anyone in preparation for your testimony here today?"

"I had a telephone conversation with Mr. Fraser and I've spoken with Bill."

"What did you and Mr. Fraser discuss?"

Don Fraser objected, saying their conversations were protected by attorney-client privilege. Once again, our discovery master, Linda Porter, stepped in.

"Have you made arrangements for Mr. Fraser to represent you here today, Mr. Collins?" Linda asked.

Thomas cleared his throat. "I assumed that because he was representing Bill, he would be representing me as well."

"Were any specific arrangements made for representation today?" she followed up.

"No, not specifically," Thomas replied. "But that was my general understanding based on experience where the company attorney represents all the principals in these proceedings."

I said, "Perhaps we can clear this up with a few more general questions."

After getting a nod from Linda, I asked Thomas, "Have you ever, in any litigation, had your deposition taken and been advised by your company attorney to consult your own attorney?"

Thomas thought for a while. "You mean with a suggestion of possible conflict of interest between the company and me?"

"Yes, that would be one such situation."

He hesitated. "Yes. A couple of times I'd been named separately and the company attorney suggested I hire an outside attorney."

"Did you?"

"No. I thought I knew enough to stay out of trouble."

"Did Mr. Fraser advise you to consult with your own attorney before coming here today?"

"No. We didn't talk about it."

"Have you paid any money to Mr. Fraser?"

"I paid Mr. Fraser for Bill's invoices over the last six months."

"When did that start?"

"Sometime in February, I think."

"Since this is August, that is six months. Have you seen a bill for each month until now?"

"Yes."

"Have you signed any agreements with Mr. Fraser to be responsible for Bill's legal expenses?"

"No. I have simply been paying them."

"Has Mr. Fraser, at any time, done any legal work specifically for you?"

"No."

"At your direction?"

"No."

I turned to Linda. "Ms. Porter, it seems to me that Thomas Collins is simply a percipient witness with no reasonable expectation of liability or representation by Mr. Fraser. So, there should be no application of privilege to their conversations."

"I agree. You may continue your examination," she said.

"The question was, Mr. Collins, 'What did you and Mr. Fraser discuss in preparation for your testimony today?'"

"We talked about Bill's job prospects and the fact that I've been loaning him money. And the arrangements for me to be here today."

"Did you discuss the Vistamont property?"

"No."

"Did you discuss the criminal proceeding?"

"Only that we were both glad it was over and that Bill didn't have to go to prison."

"Nothing about how Bill got such a light sentence?"

"No."

"Mr. Fraser didn't ask you about the sentence?"

"No. And I couldn't have told him anything anyway. That was all Paladino."

"Have you asked Mr. Paladino about the sentence?"

"No. Only to say we were grateful."

Disappointed that I hadn't gotten anything more of importance, I took a deep breath and continued.

"Mr. Collins, what is your position at Collins Construction?" I asked.

"I own and operate the company."

"Is it a corporation?"

"Yes."

"Who else is on the board?"

"My wife, Mary and my eldest son, Robert."

"What positions do they hold?"

"Mary is the secretary; Robert is the treasurer."

"Did Bill ever hold a position on the board?"

"No."

"How many people are employed by Collins Construction?"

"Full time, about 50. Part time and temporary, another 100—give or take."

"Has Bill worked for Collins Construction?"

"Yes."

"Can you tell me what positions Bill has held and the timeframes for each?"

"He has worked as general labor off and on since he was in high school."

"Was he recently employed there?"

"Yes. He was doing general labor until late March or early April—I don't remember."

"Was he ever a full-time employee?"

"No."

"How was he classified?"

"Temporary."

"What does that mean?"

"He might be getting 25-40 hours per week as a short-term hire."

"What kind of duties would he have had?"

"Whatever the foreman at the job site asked him to do. It could be carpentry, foundation digging, running a Cat—a Caterpillar tractor or grader—or hauling water in buckets. He could have been smoothing concrete. As I said, whatever the foreman told him to do."

"When is your busy season?"

"If the sun is out, we're busy."

"Did something happen that caused Bill not to be working for you now?"

"Yes."

"Please explain."

"A couple of my foremen said they didn't want him on their crews."

"Did they say why?"

"Something to do with his attitude."

"Is he eligible for rehire?"

"If a foreman wants him."

"Can you tell me anything about Bill's attitude problem?"

"Not really. We have a lot of people coming through our crews. I have great foremen. If they like someone, he stays. If they don't want to work with someone, he goes."

"How would Bill go about getting rehired?"

"He'd have to ask one of the foremen to add him to a crew."

"Is there always room for one more?"

"Almost always. Like I said, there are a lot of comings and goings."

"If he were to be rehired, what would his wage be?"

"General labor starts at $15-20 per hour. Cat drivers make more. Concrete pumpers and finishers also make more. Master carpenters make more."

"Is Bill qualified for more than general labor?"

"He knows how to do all of those things, but we run a union shop and there might be some seniority issues for him to be hired as more than general labor."

"Do you ever see him as more than general labor?" I mentally crossed my fingers, hopeful that Bill could earn more money in the future as part of the executive team.

"Possibly."

"Depending on what?"

"Performance, recommendations from the foremen."

"If he buckled down, he could advance in the company?"

"Yes." At least Thomas seemed honest in his approach.

"Is this generally a good time for construction?"

"Yes. Things normally slow down a little after Thanksgiving, but we have crews working year-round. If it is raining, we generally have some interior finishing work to be done."

"But to be clear, if Bill made nice with just one of your foremen, he could be hired quickly?"

"Yes."

"Let's talk about Bill's arrest in February. Was that the first time, to your knowledge, that Bill was arrested?"

"No."

"When was the first time Bill was arrested that you know about?"

"I think he was a junior in high school."

"What was he arrested for?"

"He got into a fight at school." It was the first time Thomas showed any discomfort.

"Can you describe what happened?"

"It would all be hearsay."

"How so?"

"The information came from his coach."

"Let's see where this goes. What did the coach tell you?"

Don shifted and started to sputter. I cut him off. "I only want to know what was said—not whether it was true or not. That will come later."

Linda repeated my question to Thomas. "What did the coach tell you?"

Thomas looked at her, then at Don, then at Bill. He clenched and unclenched his jaw. "The coach told me that Bill lost his wrestling match. When the meet was over, he found the boy that had beaten him and sucker-punched the kid. Broke his nose."

"Then what?"

"The boys all started to get into it, but the coaches got control in a hurry."

"But the police were called?"

"Yes, the other boy's parents were there and made the call."

"What happened with the police?" I asked.

"Bill was taken to the station near the Hall of Justice. Mary and I went there and met with the cops. After some talking, they let him go with a warning."

"Was there any kind of lawsuit?"

"No."

"Did you or anybody on Bill's behalf give money to the boy whose nose was broken?"

"Yes."

"Who gave the money?"

"Me."

"How much did you give them?"

"$2,000."

"Did Bill pay you back?"

"No."

"Does he still owe you for that?"

"Technically, no. But it hasn't been forgotten."

"When was the next time Bill was arrested?"

"I think it was a couple of years later. He was out of high school and going to West Valley Junior College."

"What happened this time?"

"A DUI."

"How old was he?"

"I think he was 21. So 1976 or 1977. He said he'd been at a house party and there was a keg. At least nobody got hurt."

"Was he booked?"

"Yes. He spent the night in lockup and was released the next day."

"How was it resolved?"

"I think the lawyer we hired said something about pleading Bill to a 'wet reckless.' Some kind of special plea."

"Was there a penalty?" I asked.

"Yes. He had to spend a few weekends picking up trash on the roadsides and pay a fine."

"How much was the fine?"

"$500, plus costs."

"Did you advance the $500?"

"Yes."

"Does he still owe you for that?"

Thomas looked at Bill. "Yes."

"And the lawyer?"

"Yes."

"Who was the lawyer?"

"Robert Paladino."

"The same lawyer who represented him in February of this year?"

"Yes."

"Did you pay him too?"

"Yes."

"How much did he charge?"

"$2,000."

"When was the next time, to your knowledge, that Bill was arrested?"

"This past February."

"This was the arrest for spousal battery on Carol?"

"I think that is what they said."

Now I asked what I really wanted to know. "Do you have any information about how the charges were reduced from a felony to a misdemeanor?"

"The lawyer said they made a plea deal."

"Robert Paladino?"

"Yes."

"With whom was the deal made?"

"He just said he was able to talk to the DA and get the charges reduced."

"Did he say who the DA was he talked with?"

"Maybe. I don't remember."

"Have you made any political contributions to the DA?"

"We make political contributions to most of the city and county people."

"How much did you give the DA?"

"I truly don't remember. Probably about $1,000, but that's a guess."

"Do you know if Bill has been arrested any other times?"

"No."

"How much did you pay the lawyer to represent Bill on the spousal battery case?"

"$7,000."

"So Bill owes you for that, too?"

Again, he looked at Bill. "Yes." No animus, just a look.

"Was there a fine?"

"Yes. $2,000."

"Did you pay that as well?"

"Yes."

"Are you also putting that on his tab?"

"That is one way to put it."

"OK. Let's talk about Vistamont. Do you remember when Bill and Carol moved into the house on Vistamont in San Jose?"

"I think Bill had been there since sometime in 1982. I think Carol moved in sometime that winter before Joey was born."

"Were you ever on the title to that house?"

"Yes. We—Mary and I—bought it as a rental sometime in the '70s. I remember that Bill was finished at West Valley and was working construction. He needed a place to stay, so we rented it to him."

"Was he ever on the title?"

"Why don't you do your job and get a title report? Sorry. I'm sure you already have it. Yes, we added Bill as a tenant-in-common when he and Carol got married."

"And now?"

"He's off."

"What happened?"

"He wasn't working, he wasn't making the payments. He kept asking Mary and me for money. We started loaning him money and making the monthly payments on the house ourselves. After a few months, we asked him to sign it back to us and we rented it to another family."

"Did you have Carol sign any papers relating to that house?"

"Yes."

"What were they?"

"If I remember correctly, there was an agreement that she would not be able to claim any interest in the house."

"Was she advised to see an attorney?"

"I don't know. Our attorney prepared a document. I gave it to Bill. Bill gave it back to me with Carol's notarized signature."

"Did you give Bill anything for the equity built up during the time he had been there and making payments?"

"We gave him some kind of credit toward the loans and past expenses we'd kept track of."

"Is there some kind of ledger with credits and debits for all of these amounts?"

"Yes. I think Mary has it somewhere." I heard Don suck in air when Thomas made that response.

"When was the last time you gave him any money?"

"We *loaned* him another $2,000 last month. But we told him that was the end of it. No more."

"Do you know of other contractors who are hiring?"

"Yes."

"Have you encouraged Bill to apply to any of them?"

"Yes."

"Do you know whether he has?"

"No. I would expect that if he had, I or one of my foremen would have received a call. Nobody has told me anything about him applying."

"Do you have any kind of arrangement for him to get back into Vistamont?"

"No."

"Some other place?"

"No."

"How much older than Bill is Robert?"

"Five years."

"So Robert is about 36 years old?"

"He is 37."

"Close enough. But he is the treasurer of Collins Construction?"

"Yes. He went straight through college and got an MBA at Santa Clara University. He has worked summers at Collins Construction since high school and through undergraduate and grad school."

"Did you help him buy a house?"

"Yes. When he and his wife got married, we gave them a down payment on their house."

"Were you on title to that house, at any time?"

"No."

"How much time does Joey spend at your house?"

"I don't know exactly. He's there most days, but I can't tell you hours."

"How would you say, as his grandfather, he is at interacting with Bill?"

"OK, I guess."

"How does Joey act when Bill comes into your house to pick him up?"

"I'm rarely there when that happens."

"Does Michelle spend much time at your house?"

"I think she comes over to drop off or pick up Joey. She comes when we have everybody over for BBQ and swim parties in the summer. I haven't spent that much time with her."

"When you have these BBQ and swim parties, have you seen her with Joey?"

"Yes."

"I understand that Joey is not yet potty-trained. If he has a wet or dirty diaper, does he go to Bill or Michelle?"

"I think he goes to whichever of them is nearest at the time."

"When Bill and Carol were still married, did she join the family at these parties?"

"Yes."

"At any of these parties did you see Joey in any kind of distress?"

"What do you mean?"

"If Joey had a diaper issue or had fallen and was in distress, did you see him go to Carol or Bill?"

"I don't remember Carol ever letting him out of her sight, so my best recollection is that he would have been closest to her. But I have seen Bill change his diapers."

"Have you seen Bill discipline Joey?"

"Yes."

"What caused the need for discipline?"

"With a two-year-old? Are you kidding me? It could be throwing a pebble, fighting with a cousin, or just needing a nap. Crying for another cookie. You name it."

"And how would Bill react?"

Don just said, with a bored tone, "Objection, vague."

Linda stepped in. "Please be more specific, Mr. Gregory. And how much longer do you expect to be with this witness?"

"I'm almost done," I said. "Just a few more minutes. Mr. Collins, did you ever see Bill give Joey any kind of discipline?"

"Yes."

"Did he ever yell at Joey?"

"Yes, but I think it happened when Joey would do something requiring an immediate response, like yelling 'Stop!' before something bad could happen. Two-year-old stuff."

"Did you ever see Bill strike Joey?"

"Yes. Joey was hitting our dog with a stick. Bill took it away and spanked Joey on the bottom. I'd have spanked him too."

"Did Joey ever complain to you that Bill had hurt his wrist?"

"No."

"Have you ever noticed Joey with any kind of injury?"

"Yes. He's a little kid. He runs. He falls. He scrapes his knees and the palms of his hands."

"Let's go back to the ledger you say Mary keeps on your financial arrangements with Bill. I'd like to see that and ask a few questions about it. There are a couple of ways to get that done. The easiest would be for you to call Mary and have her fax it to us now so we can finish this deposition. Or, we could subpoena her to appear for her deposition and bring the ledger—"

Thomas cut me off. "Let me give her a call and see if we can't get this done and over with, and not bother Mary."

"It's time for a break anyway," Linda said. "So let's see if Mr. Collins can get the exhibit and avoid further disruption for everybody. OK, Mr. Collins?"

We all got up and stretched. We left Thomas in the conference room to call Mary. I wrote out our fax number for him to give to her. Fifteen minutes later, after using the restrooms and refilling coffee cups, we were back in the conference room. Mary had indeed faxed a copy of the spreadsheet. It was a single sheet of ledger paper. I had Thomas identify it, initial the page, and explain the headers.

Then I asked him, "Can you show me where there was any credit for equity in the Vistamont house?"

He looked at the sheet for a moment. "No. I don't see it."

"As an owner, do you have any opinion as to the increase in value for that property between 1980 and 1985?"

He looked at the ceiling as he made some mental calculations. "Probably $45-50,000. Best guess. We paid about $70,000 for it and it is now probably worth between $115-120,000."

"And during those years, did Bill make all of the payments on the house?"

"Yes."

"Principal, interest, taxes, insurance, and utilities?"

"Yes."

"And for the record, the amount your ledger shows you having lent Bill is $30,000, including the various attorneys' fees and fines?"

"Yes."

"That's all I have for now. Thank you, Mr. Collins."

Everybody was tired at this point. I asked to talk to Don briefly in my office about our timing. In private, I said I didn't think I needed anything more from Bill at that point and would it be OK to just take his follow-up deposition off calendar and reschedule it with Linda should we need to go forward. He agreed if he could do the same with Carol's. We went back into the conference room, put our agreement on the record, and made the arrangements with Linda, should we need her again.

* * * * *

"Why didn't you take Bill's deposition that day?" Harris asked.

"Because I didn't think there was anything I'd get from him that I hadn't gotten from Michelle or Thomas. And I didn't want to give up another opportunity to question him, should something come up!"

"And Don didn't want more from Carol?"

"Good thinking. Don was in the same place I was. The only thing he'd want to follow up on was her ability to work, but he could see she was still wearing the collar and that would be a turn-off for any likely employer looking for someone with her current job skills."

"So, this way you both get another chance later? Makes sense."

* * * * *

I got to the office a little late the next day. On my desk, there was another arrangement of flowers waiting for me. This time the card read: "Let's exchange fantasies!" There was no signature. I just left a message with Diane Gold. And smiled as I thought that my next fantasy would involve Sarah.

43 - Motion to Consolidate in General Civil Court

October 2, 1985

After the depositions of Michelle Barnes and Thomas Collins, Marty and I discussed how we were going to proceed. The most time efficient, we determined, was to set the cases for trial together. Consolidation such as this was an established legal principle: all matters in conflict between the same individuals should be handled in the same legal proceeding, avoiding what is known as a multiplicity of actions.

But that required an application to the court to formally consolidate the two proceedings. We had never done this before, but it made sense to us.

We decided the application should first be made to the department that assigned personal injury cases. The motion calendar the day we appeared was assigned to Judge Jacob Perazzo, in the main courthouse on Market Street. Judge Perazzo was in Department 8 on the third floor. These are large courtrooms with brick walls on the sides and dark maple paneling behind the judge's bench, which is two steps up from the main floor. The flags of the United States and the State of California stand behind the bench. There are seats for about a hundred spectators, but today, as is typical for the motion calendar, it was standing room only. Even the jury box on the right side of the courtroom was filled with lawyers. The witness stand sat between the judge's bench and the jury box, and a railing separated the counsel tables from the spectators' seats.

I was surprised that Don Fraser came in to represent Bill. I'd never known Don to work on a personal injury case. Both Marty and I announced our appearances when our case was finally called.

Judge Perazzo said he'd read our papers and asked if we had anything different to add. Neither attorney had anything.

"I know the rules favor efficiency by having all matters between two individuals be decided in a single proceeding," the judge said. "But I'm having trouble with the concept of joining a Family Court matter, which is not to be tried by a jury, with a personal injury case that is being tried to a jury. Mr. Gregory, how do you see that working?"

I wanted to scream that it had all been explained in our papers. Sensing my frustration, Marty put a hand on my shoulder, rose to his feet, and addressed the bench in a calm tone of voice that I wouldn't have possibly been able to muster.

"In every jury case I've seen or been a part of, Your Honor, the judge has made any number of findings and rulings without the input of a jury. I've even seen a judge make a directed finding of liability. So I would expect to put out all of the evidence on the injury case. Mr. Gregory would do the same with the divorce case. The trial judge would make the decisions on property division, support, and custody while the jury would decide liability and damages relative to the injuries. Since the parties are the same and the key experts are the same for damages and support, this would be the most efficient use of the time and resources for all involved. Of course there is an added advantage: should there be a verdict for the plaintiff, Carol Collins, the judge could award assets at the same time that would help satisfy the judgment." He resumed his seat.

Judge Perazzo thought for a moment and turned to Don for his response.

"Your Honor," Don said, rising, "it would be wrong for the people—that is, the jury—who are deciding damage to first see what assets are available to the defendant. The concept is prejudicial." He stayed on his feet, an expression of disbelief painted on his face.

The judge turned back to us.

This time I stood and spoke. "In a divorce, the parties in California remain fiduciaries until the divorce is granted and the property divided. After that, they don't owe any particular duty to each other. Isn't it prejudicial for a defendant, without any duty to the plaintiff, to be able to dispose of all their assets in advance of an award? We believe that the defendant in this case has already started doing that and we want to have something left in the kitty for when we receive the judgment."

Marty stood up and added, "Besides Your Honor, in cases involving potential punitive damages, the jury hears about the assets of the defendant."

"Your Honor," Don raised his hand. "There is another matter involved. Mr. Collins would like to have his divorce this year. It is already October. I've prepared a motion to bifurcate the divorce so Mr. Collins will be single by December 31st. His fiduciary obligation will continue until the property is divided, which shouldn't take more than another three or four months. Since I don't think the injury case could find a courtroom this year, the arguments by Mr. Cramer and Mr. Gregory are moot and would create an unwarranted hardship on Mr. Collins."

The judge nodded. "Mr. Gregory, I understand your predicament, but there is no way the injury case could find a civil courtroom this year. And maybe not even next year. We have too many cases that, according to law, must be tried this year.

Perhaps a Family Court judge may be willing to take it on. I'm going to deny your motion, without prejudice to having it renewed in Family Court."

Disappointed, I wondered what it would take for one of these guys to extend their comfort zones, just a little.

44 - Motion to Consolidate in Family Court

November 14, 1985

It took six more weeks to get our hearing in the Family Court at Park Avenue and Almaden Road. Bill's motion for bifurcation was heard at the same time. While Judge DePalma agreed with my various points, he challenged my request.

"Look around, Mr. Gregory," the judge said. "We have a jury box, but no deliberation rooms. No jury restrooms. No jury space. While I'm sympathetic to the potential loss of access to assets, I'm not prepared to deny a bifurcation or delay a division of assets. So, how would you have me make this happen?"

"Your Honor," I answered, "this courthouse is close enough in proximity to the main courthouse that the jury pool could assemble there and then be sent here. Or, conversely, not all the courtrooms at Market Street are busy the entire month of December. Some will be dark. Would it not be conceivable to make arrangements with the presiding judge to use one of them? I think every judge here at Park has at one time or another been assigned to Market. They wouldn't get lost. There is plenty of parking."

Judge DePalma shook his head. "Mr. Gregory, you are suggesting a great disruption in two court buildings. I'm sorry if it causes some inconvenience for the parties and the witnesses, but I'm going to grant the motion for bifurcation, dissolving the marriage effective December 31st, 1985, and deny your motion for consolidation. The best I can do is set a settlement conference for Thursday, December 12th, at 9:30 a.m. And Mr. Fraser, prepare the paperwork accordingly."

The judge may as well have said to me, "Don't let the door hit you in the ass on your way out."

I was very close to blurting something that would have had me held in contempt of court, but I held my temper. I had too many cases in front of Judge DePalma that would have been badly affected if I threw a tantrum.

However, I stalked back to my office as fast as I could to work off my anger.

Hearing the news, Marty offered what little support he could. "You knew it was a long shot," Marty said. "That's why we started in General Civil. But let's just play it out."

Carol hadn't come to court for the motion, so I had to pull myself together before calling her. She took the bad news better than I had. "I never really expected it to happen," she said with an audible sigh. "You never see it on TV, and if it were possible, they would have had it on TV!"

* * * * *

"Is it always like this?" Harris looked pained. "Judge DePalma gives you a little victory then comes back and smacks you. Doesn't that hurt?"

I had to smile. "If you are thinking about working with people in the legal system, you have to get used to that. Besides there being two sides to every story, it takes a lot out of you to keep coming back when you get knocked down. I told you there are multiple reasons this case was memorable."

"But still...I'm not sure I'd want to have to get used to losing in court like that. Does Uncle Marty have those problems, too?"

"Uncle Marty loses some motions, and even some trials. Remember what I said about lawyers who say they win every time?"

It didn't take him long to recall. "You mean, 'they only take sure winners and don't take any risks'?"

"That's pretty close," I said, nodding. "But think about it: if you win at least half of your marginal cases, you can feel pretty good about helping people. And, I believe, it makes for a better lawyer. As far as Marty goes, I think he shakes things off more easily than I do. That is one reason I quit doing cases with insurance companies. But that's another story for another time."

45 - Settling the Divorce

December 12, 1985

Settlement conferences in Family Court can make you crazy. They are usually managed by experienced attorneys who volunteer to act as pro tem judges to try and get the sides to settle. I volunteered for this duty about every three months. Pro tems sometimes get the department judge to answer hypothetically posed questions so the judge cannot be said to have pre-judged an issue in advance of a hearing and the presentation of evidence, but by and large the attorneys and parties are on their own.

I prepared my documents for the settlement conference, and wrote out our concepts of the way a division would work, the custody plan, and support amounts for children and alimony. Don and I swapped documents one week before the actual conference, as directed, to give each of us the opportunity to talk further with our clients, now faced with hard realities.

Carol and I arrived at Family Court before Don—no surprise there. We got scanned by security and I put Carol in what was the last available cubicle to make sure we had a semi-private space for when the work would begin. I hated having to use a bench out in the open area.

Don and Bill came in a little later. Don motioned Bill to sit on the other side of the main room, and Don and I entered Judge DePalma's courtroom. The judge, of course, was not there. His clerk noted the time we arrived, and informed us the Collins case had been assigned to Pro Tem Edward Miller. Ed sat in the jury box, reading what I assumed to be the thick case file. A longtime friend and a California Certified Family Law Specialist, I was happy with our assigned pro tem. Ed knew his stuff and wouldn't suffer any foolishness.

Ed rose and shook our hands, told us he had skimmed through our proposals, and wanted to meet with each of us and our clients. We retreated to the cubicle Carol held, signed the papers authorizing him to act as pro tem, and he then asked that Carol and Bill go to opposite sides of the main floor while he talked to the attorneys. I escorted Carol to a safe area far away from Bill, pointed out the restroom door, and promised to check back as soon as possible.

I returned to the cubicle where Don and Ed waited. Ed asked me how I expected Bill to pay support for Carol and Joey. I pointed out the information from the depositions showing Bill should be working, earning $15 per hour, 40 hours per week, which equaled $600 per week. Carol, on the other hand was just now cleared to go back to work where she could make $3.50 per hour, 35 hours per week, or $122 per week. We'd used the same budget we put together for our first hearing, $1,500 per month, meaning Carol would need roughly $1,700 per month in pre-tax cash flow to make ends meet. I also pointed out the original ruling by Judge DePalma to make support retroactive to April 5 and his interim order of $1,225 per month.

As to division of assets, with no savings or investments found, only junk for furniture, and an obvious award of the cars they were driving to each of them with no offsets, Ed wondered what we were doing there.

An updated custody report from Kathryn Monahan said Carol was now physically and emotionally ready for a substantial amount of time with Joey. We asked for sole custody, due to the abuse.

Don, of course, acted unimpressed. "There is nothing in Monahan's report that comes close to suggesting that she is capable or that it would be in Joey's best interests to spend full time with her. Moreover, Joey clearly has a bond with Bill and Bill has proven to be capable of caring for him."

Ed asked me to leave so he and Don could have a conversation. I walked over to where I had left Carol, made sure she was OK, and told her what was going on. After about 15 minutes, Don found us and said Ed wanted to talk to me; he had some things to discuss with Bill.

Ed was very direct, as expected. "Steve, I sympathize with your situation. I get it—you are stuck in a case without being paid, the husband is a dick, and there seems no way out. There is no real money to pay support or damages; and child sharing is awful. Does that sum it up?"

"Yes. But if I get Bill on the stand the judge will hate him and try to make things right."

"You know you can't afford to try this case over back support and custody." Trust Ed to be blunt about the business realities, too.

"So, what do you propose?"

He looked at his notes. "I've told Don to talk to Bill about this settlement: Child sharing: 50-50, on a three-day/four-day schedule starting this Friday evening, December 13th at 6 p.m. Joey stays with Carol until Monday night and shifting each month. If the parties cannot agree on how this will work you can contact Monahan directly for a referral to a child sharing special master. Support: $750 per month in child support, $500 per month in spousal support for three years, all retroactive to April 5th. Child support to continue after three years at the rate of

$1,150 per month. Actual payments to begin December 16th. Payments on arrears of $5,250 for family support will begin on December 16th and then on the 15th of each month thereafter in the amount of $500. The $5,250 will be considered family support and thus deductible to Bill, and taxable to Carol. Property division: each will keep their personal belongings and automobiles. The court will reserve jurisdiction over the question of any credits Bill is entitled to from his family relating to equity in the Vistamont house. Is there anything I've left out?"

"Where is the cash coming from? What about attorney's fees?"

"Apparently, he has made nice with one of the foremen at Collins Construction. He'll start work on Monday. As to how much he's making, he says $22 per hour. He'll borrow some more from his family to get things started. As to attorney's fees and costs, I note your request for $30,000. While I don't doubt that figure has actually been earned, you know Judge DePalma won't give it to you. You have two options: one, take $5,000 now in a lump sum; or two, submit letter briefs to Judge DePalma. Which do you prefer?"

"Let me talk to Carol. Give me a few minutes."

"Reconvene in 15?"

I nodded and took my notes to Carol. It looked like there were tear stains on her blue dress. Her eyes and nose were red. I explained Ed's proposal.

"If we do this, I won't have to testify in court?" she asked.

"That's right."

"What do you recommend?"

"Thinking it through, there is not much more we'd get by having a trial. And we wouldn't have a trial this year, anyway.

Maybe not until February or March of next year. So the support and property division looks fair to me. I am really worried about the attorney's fees and costs. You saw the breakdown I put in the settlement conference statement? There is more than $50,000 owed, including my time, Linda Porter, Dr. Diane Gold, the court reporters, and my investigator."

She gnawed on her lip, obviously uncertain. "So what happens if you only get $5,000 from Bill?"

"You will owe me the rest. That is in our contract."

"I don't know how I'll be able to pay you."

"Will your family help?"

"You heard my mom. She put up $5,000 to begin with and said no more. I believe she meant that." She paused. "What about the personal injury case?"

"If Bill had the resources, the P.I. case could be worth four to five hundred thousand dollars. Unfortunately, we can't show assets that would justify that kind of verdict—or that we could collect on it if we got it." I added, "There will also be more attorney fees to make that case."

She sniffled and sat quietly. I just waited. Finally she said, "Let's take it. I guess I'll owe you a lot of money."

I found Ed and Don in the cubicle. Ed looked at me, a question on his face.

"What happened with Bill?" I asked first.

"He's not happy," Don said. "But that is what settlements are about. He thinks the support is out of the question and almost threw up when I told him he'd have to pay you $5,000. But, in the end, he agreed to the package."

"Yeah," I said. "In the end, so did she."

We went into the courtroom and recited the agreement before Judge DePalma with the court reporter taking down the details. I agreed to write it up, circulate the signatures, and submit it to the court for formalization.

Carol was quiet as we walked back to my office. I explained that, as we had wrapped up the divorce, I would ask the court for a trial date for the injury case.

Finishing a case as emotional as this one, I had no energy left for work that afternoon. Marty and I had lunch at Manny's Cellar and discussed plans for Carol's injury case. Don had filed a response to the complaint we'd filed, so we could tell the court we were ready to go to trial. We decided that we would not need to do any more depositions, so the budget had to cover the neurosurgeon, Dr. Anton and the psychologist, Dr. Gold. From experience we could expect $2,500 for each of them for their testimony. The defense would have to pay for the experts' time at depositions—if the defense took their depositions.

After explaining the paperwork to Sue, I'd had enough for the day, and headed home where I could take Timbur out for a nice walk and clear my head.

The next morning I was in early to catch up on my other cases and review what Sue had done on the Collins case. At 11 o'clock, Sue came in with a big grin. She was carrying another flower arrangement, this time from Hill's. She'd obviously read the card, which said: "Let's do dinner. I'll bring the whip."

I laughed. "Sarah's going to love the flowers. I'm not sure about the whip."

I was right: she liked the flowers—I think she was getting used to them. She declined the whip.

46 - The Drama Triangle

April 2, 1986

There were no requests for discovery from either side and a trial date was set for the week of Monday, May 19, 1986. On April 2, our mail brought a "Notice of Substitution of Attorney" that showed William Collins as attorney in place of Donald Fraser. This meant that Bill was listed as his own attorney with his address and phone.

So I called Bill, not the least surprised when Bill explained that since he couldn't pay Don, Don had quit, and had Bill sign the substitution. The California Rules of Professional Conduct prevent attorneys from quitting a case that has a pending trial date, without a judge's permission. When I asked Bill about getting the judge's permission, he shrugged it off.

"That's OK," Bill said. "Nobody else wants to take the case and I'm not going to make him work any more for free."

Marty had been preparing for the jury trial, so I went to him with the news. "Hmm," he said. "If Bill doesn't want to pay for a jury, do we? I think at this stage, I'd rather not advance the jury fees. Let's revisit this when the fee deposit date comes."

"That sounds right," I said. "If we get a big judgment, do you think Don should be liable to Bill?"

Marty grinned. "To me, it's clearly an ethical violation to bail on a client at this stage of a case without making a motion to continue the trial. But malpractice? Maybe. It's not a slam dunk. It would probably depend on the size of the award."

"Yes," I said. "But it would sure be nice to be the third-party-beneficiaries of a large malpractice award. And I wouldn't mind seeing Don suffer a bit for the way he has supported Bill. I've never understood how, even after the criminal case was resolved, Don wouldn't have been up-front and attempted to resolve the injury case."

"Come on, partner," Marty chuckled. "You know he can't do that without an OK from the client!"

I shrugged. "Yes, I know. But when I've represented someone accused of abuse, we've been able to minimize the conflict through apology and compromise."

"And how many times have you had a client who broke someone's neck?" Marty asked.

"Zip," I replied. "You're right. I've had a few cases where the violence has been really minor in comparison to this case. It is something to think about: what would have happened if Don and Bill had come up with an apology and a few extra dollars? But they fought everything."

"Get over yourself! You're never going to change the way the world works for guys like Bill. Now get out of here, I've got some more work to do. Let's grab a beer later."

"Deal!"

I called Diane to talk about Don's withdrawal and our other trial preparation.

"I don't think we've talked about this case since October," I began. "How is that possible?"

Her reply was typical Diane. "I guess you didn't miss me enough!"

"True. Did you even hear about Bill's criminal case and his girlfriend?"

"Carol only said that you got her to come in for the deposition. I didn't have any of the details."

I filled her in on the plea deal and Michelle's stories about how Bill had been abusing her before leaving for Carol, then seemingly enjoying it when he returned to her.

"That is total bullshit!" Diane exclaimed. "He is a sadist and is going to kill someone—it is only a matter of time. Michelle is in real danger and having a 'safe word' isn't enough!" I heard her doing some controlled breathing before she asked, "Has he isolated her the way he did Carol?"

"I didn't follow up on it," I replied, sheepishly. "I was just happy to have established a pattern of abusive behavior."

"Well, here's the deal," she said. "Bill, like most abusers, drove a wedge between Carol and her family. That made her more vulnerable to his control. Once isolated from her family, Bill controlled her finances and more of her life, making her dependent on him and afraid to leave. But you knew that. What we didn't know is the extent to which this was a pattern for him."

"Gee, I was just trying to get something to impeach him in court. It seems Michelle confirms it as a pattern. That seems to mean more to you, doesn't it?"

"It means that he's undoubtedly done this before. He probably started forcing himself on girls in high school or even earlier. Anybody that gets sexually excited at causing other people pain could be capable of killing someone at one time or another. He came close to making Carol a quadriplegic. The system really let Carol down and now someone else is going to suffer."

I agreed. "Even the ADA was apologetic about how Bill managed to get the deal that he did. I have no idea what we can do now that would make a difference in the criminal case."

Silence. Apparently Diane was as stumped as I was.

"You know, Diane, when I started this call, I was thinking about how I would love to withdraw the same as Don," I confessed. "This case has been making me crazy. Literally. Plus, we've taken a financial beating on this case and don't think there's ever going to be a payout—in money or closure for Carol."

Diane laughed. "Don't discount the value of closure. I'm not getting paid either. Nothing since the $7,500 from the State Fund. But I can't let you quit."

"How could you stop me?"

"First, I'd go to Sarah and explain that if you didn't get Carol her final day in court, Carol would probably kill herself."

"Suicide? Really? I thought she was doing much better, making progress every day."

"She was for a while, but now she's back to hanging on by a thread. She is doing better with Joey, but that's wearing her out. She is seriously depressed and anxious. I've arranged for her to be on some anti-depressant medication, but she is looking forward to you finally slaying her dragon, as she calls it, so she can move forward. Even though we've each taken a bad hit financially, we are going to be there to see it through."

As I sat there thinking about the implications if I were to withdraw, Diane said, "There is something else, too."

"What's that?" I asked, adding to myself, besides pissing off my partner and my wife.

"Have we talked about what's called the Drama Triangle? Persecutor, victim, rescuer?"

"Not that I recall."

"Well," she said, "in relationships like this there is a persecutor—Bill; a victim—Carol; and a rescuer—you. As the victim, Carol's relationship experience is mostly with that kind of dynamic. Her mother was her first persecutor, then Bill rescued her, later turning into a persecutor. The short answer is that when you rescue her from Bill the persecutor, she may well assume a new role—not as a victim." She paused, as if letting that sink in. "There have already been boundary questions in this relationship, so she may—I repeat, may—become a persecutor herself. And guess who might become the victim." After a moment of my silence, she said, "It's not Joey."

"She's going to physically beat on me?" I asked, incredulous.

"No," Diane said. "But she could make a false allegation about you to the Bar. Or to Sarah."

"If that's supposed to make me want to continue, it's not encouraging. I'd like to think that you'd testify on my behalf. And where does that mean Bill the persecutor turns his attention?"

"First, you know you don't want to fight with the State Bar. Second, regarding Bill, from what you've told me about his relationship with Michelle, he has been defused, for now. I don't see you at any direct risk from him. But if you don't follow through with the trial, I won't have the continued time with her to re-direct her actions, and you'd be more at risk from her than from Bill. As it is, I think I can work with her on boundaries and behaviors toward you and let you know if I believe there is any danger of her escalating toward you." After some hesitation she went on. "Is there any chance that the judge in the civil case will be able to step in to change the consequences for Bill?"

"I wish. The only thing I can think of is punitive damages and a stern lecture. Could that create some awareness?"

"Pigs will fly before a lecture will change Bill. I'd bet you a trip to Maui he's had plenty of lectures already."

She'd done me many favors on this case and others, so, after some hesitation, I agreed to stay on for the trial.

47 - Personal Injury Settlement Conference

May 15, 1986

As a cost containment measure, Marty and I had decided not to advance the jury fees, and therefore forewent the option of a jury trial. Usually, in personal injury cases, there is an insurance company that will advance the fees for the defense with a deadline of two weeks in advance of the trial date. In our case, however, Bill wasn't covered by liability insurance, so we instead took our chances on a settlement conference. That left Marty free to work on some other cases, and me to represent Carol at the injury trial.

Without an attorney to represent him, we were not concerned about Bill and his ability to cross-examine either Diane or Carol. We'd also planned to save money and not call Dr. Anton. Rather, we would let Diane include Dr. Anton's earlier report as part of the basis for her opinion regarding causation and the injuries suffered by Carol.

As with the divorce case, the sides were required to exchange settlement conference statements one week before the actual settlement conference, the Thursday before the trial date. The statement must include a discussion of the issues surrounding liability, an itemization of medical expenses, and what we were seeking in damages. We had our statement prepared and sent to Bill for expected delivery on May 8. Not surprisingly, we didn't get anything from Bill.

We showed up for the settlement conference on May 15 at the main courthouse on Market Street, across from my office. Carol wore the same blue dress she'd worn when we went to

Family Court and a lightweight cream sweater. This time she had her hair pulled back in a pony tail, yet still looked like a waif. Bill was there, alone, wearing the same outfit he'd worn at his farce of a preliminary hearing: Navy blazer, light blue oxford shirt and tan slacks.

Without a word, Bill handed me a typed page which framed the crushed vertebrae as an accident that happened during consensual sex. It declared that there should be no damage award because, first, there was no liability, and second, she had fully recovered, and lastly, the support he was paying more than made up for any loss of income.

At least Bill had been warned that settlement conferences in injury cases are also assigned to pro tem attorneys, as in Family Court. I had never worked with our assigned pro tem, David Tannenbaum, who took us into the jury room of Department 12 on the third floor of the Market Street courthouse.

Tannenbaum acknowledged receipt of the statement I'd sent in, and asked Bill why he hadn't complied and why he didn't have an attorney. Bill's excuse: he hadn't responded because he didn't know he had to, and no attorney would work with him. He gave Tannenbaum a copy of the same sheet he'd given me.

Even though I was going into the jury room with Bill and Tannenbaum, I'd offered Carol the choice of waiting in the hallway outside of the courtroom or in the courtroom, where she'd at least have a cushioned seat while we were in the back. One step into the courtroom and Carol said she'd rather wait in the hall.

Tannenbaum held true to form and started with me as representing the plaintiff, asking for a summary of the case and the state of settlement discussions. I anticipated that he would hold separate caucus meetings with Bill and me to convince each of us of the weaknesses of our respective positions and why we should settle. He began, "How do you respond to the claim that the injury was an accident during consensual sex?"

"When you hear from Dr. Diane Gold," I said, "you'll find that this was anything but consensual sex. From Bill's point of view, Carol got hurt worse than usual when he decided he wanted to have sex with her. Dr. Anton's report shows that the way the vertebrae were crushed is consistent with significant pressure applied through what is termed a full-Nelson wrestling hold. He says it is unreasonable to believe that the amount of pressure necessary to crush vertebrae could be applied accidentally. There had to be an intent to harm."

Tannenbaum looked at Bill with his eyebrows raised.

"I never meant to hurt her," Bill said.

"Are you prepared to offer any money to settle this case?" Tannenbaum asked Bill.

"I don't have any money to offer," he said.

"I see," Tannenbaum said. "It appears nobody picked up a jury and I don't think the judge will send this out to trial with a sitting judge. Would you both accept an experienced pro tem to act as the judge at trial?"

I thought for a moment. "Who and at what cost?"

He asked to be excused for a minute to check with the presiding judge. Upon return, he indicated Charles Griffen would be available next Wednesday in this courtroom. The only cost would be for a court reporter if we wanted an official transcript.

Bill said he didn't care. I asked to be excused to discuss it with Carol.

Taking a seat by her side, I told her that I knew Charles Griffen only by reputation, but that he was known as a good lawyer and an experienced temporary judge. He had tried a lot of jury cases and would be as generous as any of the judges in the courthouse. She agreed to having Griffen as our judge, but in order to make our agreement official I escorted her into the courtroom to restate it with Tannenbaum and Bill in front of the court reporter.

Before leaving the courthouse, I took Carol back into the empty main courtroom and had her sit in the witness chair and look out into the audience section. I explained that I'd be there and would question her from the table closest to the jury box, right in front of the witness box. I showed her where Bill was going to be and told her that he would have the right to ask her questions. She was clearly nervous, but calmed down as she spent a few more minutes in the witness box. Then we went back to my office for further preparation of her testimony.

My office was just across the street, but there was heavy traffic, and when we got the "WALK" sign and stepped off the curb, Carol put her left hand through my arm and covered it with her right hand. She let out a big sigh and said, "Please tell me it will be all right."

"Of course it will."

48 - Opening Statements

May 21, 1986

As part of our preparation, I'd gone over the critical issues with Diane and trusted her to do what she could to help with Carol. They were both in my office at 8:30 a.m. that Wednesday to have a last cup of coffee before going across the street to court. Carol looked like she hadn't slept, but had her long hair washed and brushed, her same blue dress was pressed. Her black flats looked like they had been recently polished. Her smile was thin.

Laying out the trial schedule, I reminded Carol that she would be our last witness, which would probably be after lunch. I would call Bill as an adverse witness first, then Diane, and finish with Carol. During the trial, she would sit to my right at the counsel table. Her father, Arnold, who had driven her to my office and was now in our waiting room, would be in the first row behind the bar for the trial. Her mother wasn't coming. Neither was her friend, Jill.

We got to the courtroom and checked in with the clerk. Bill was already sitting at his table, quite alone. Fittingly, neither of his parents were there for support. Just as an extra measure of insurance, I walked over to the bailiff and let him know about the nature of the case. He said he'd already talked with the judge and didn't anticipate any trouble. The light on his desk flashed, the sign that the judge was coming. I went back to my place.

The bailiff made the familiar announcement. "All rise! Department 8 of the Superior Court of the State of California is now in session. The Honorable Charles Griffen, Pro Tem, presiding." The judge climbed the stairs to the bench and made a motion for us to sit down. He was wearing a judicial robe, clearly basking in the power of the position. Almost six feet tall, with a full head of grey hair parted on the side, wire-rim glasses, clean-shaven and fit, he looked right out of central casting for the role. I knew he had actual judicial aspirations, not like most of us who volunteer to pro tem. We do it to stay in touch with what is happening in the court system and maybe pick up a few brownie points from the judges.

The judge had the Clerk call the calendar. "This is the case of Collins versus Collins," he said, and then recited the case number. The judge had us state our appearances, although we'd waived a court reporter.

"Steven Gregory for and with the plaintiff, Carol Collins," I said.

Bill stood and said, "William Collins, Your Honor. I'm representing myself."

Judge Griffen looked at him. "Are you sure you want to proceed without an attorney?"

"Yes," he replied. "Nobody wanted to take my case."

"Very well. Are both sides ready to proceed?"

Bill and I both said we were.

"Proceed Mr. Gregory," the judge said.

I'd known my opening statement since we had filed the complaint, so delivering it that morning felt natural.

"On the night of February 9th, 1985," I began, "Carol Collins was lying naked under the sheets of her queen-sized bed, her toddler asleep in the next room. It was a cold night, but she wasn't shivering due to the cold. She was shivering due to fear, because she knew that her husband, the defendant William "Bill" Collins, was going to be home soon and would be rough with her. She had come to expect this whenever Bill had been out drinking with his friends. She wasn't wearing anything because she also knew that if she had been wearing a nightgown, Bill would have ripped it off of her as he had many times in the past.

"I expect your first question is, if she knew she was going to be hurt, why was she still there? The answer, Your Honor, lies in the nature of the cycle of domestic violence which will be explained by Dr. Diane Gold later this morning.

"Carol will testify that she heard the door to the house open and close. She wept softly into her pillow. She heard Bill come into their bedroom and walk to the bed. She heard his shoes fall to the floor as he kicked them off. She heard his belt buckle make a pinging noise as his pants hit the floor. She felt the bed move as he got in and came up behind her. She began to tremble harder as Bill roughly put his arms around her shoulders, placing her in a wrestling hold known as a full-Nelson, and began putting pressure on her head, moving it forward and down. As he increased the pressure, she both heard the sound and felt the pain of vertebrae in her neck being crushed.

"'Please, Bill,' she said. 'I need to pee and get some lube.' He released her and she fled, naked, without even stopping for a robe or slippers, out the front door, across the street to the home of her friends, Jill and Tony D'Souza. She banged on the door, and in the moments she waited for it to be answered, she heard Bill coming out of their house, shouting for her to return home that instant.

"Jill was able to get her inside and called the police. Jill was able to close and lock the door before Bill got there. He banged on the door anyway, demanding that they turn Carol out and back to him. Jill got Carol a blanket. Carol said her neck really hurt, and they called an ambulance. While waiting, Jill and Tony helped Carol lie down on the floor and told her not to move her head or neck.

"Records will reflect that the police and the ambulance both arrived within seconds of each other at 2:34 a.m. Jill explained to them what she'd learned. While the paramedics secured Carol to a backboard, including lashing her head with straps, the police went to talk to Bill. Jill had told them about Joey being in the house and said they should bring Joey to her for the night. Carol said that was her wish as well.

"Carol was taken to Valley Medical, where she underwent emergency surgery to secure her vertebrae and was placed in a medical halo device which would hold her head steady—night and day—for the next eight weeks. The report from the neurosurgeon, Dr. Angelo Anton, will explain how close Carol came to quadriplegia or even life on a ventilator. Carol will talk about the hours of physical therapy necessary to regain strength in her neck. She will talk about the heartbreak of having to be separated from her infant son and the months before she could even let him sit on her lap.

"Your Honor, you will hear her stories of multiple rapes and injuries—perhaps the most severe injury being the psychological destruction of Carol's sense of self-worth, making her totally dependent on Bill, with nowhere to turn. We will present evidence of this, along with medical bills for surgery, treatment, physical therapy and lost wages caused by Bill Collins. At the conclusion of our evidence, we will ask for special damages, general damages, and substantial punitive damages.

"Thank you."

Judge Griffen looked at Bill. "Do you wish to make a statement?"

Bill rose to his feet, not appearing the least bit shaken. "What happened was an accident. That was part of our process—foreplay—when we had sex. This time, I guess, I put too much pressure on her. But I never intended to hurt her. We are divorced now and I pay her alimony and child support. I don't think I should have to pay her anything else." He sat down.

49 - Bill's Unexpected Testimony

May 21, 1986

Judge Griffen looked at me. "Call your first witness, Mr. Gregory."

I stood. "Your Honor, we call Bill Collins, under California Evidence Code, section 776."

"You understand, Mr. Collins," the judge said to Bill, "that the plaintiff may call you as a hostile witness under the California Evidence Code?"

Bill nodded. "I expected to tell my story," he said.

The judge said, "Please come to the witness stand." Bill walked to the witness box. The clerk swore him in and the judge had him take the chair.

"Mr. Collins," I began, "you just told us that what happened to Carol's neck was an accident, is that right?"

"Yes."

"But that wasn't always your story, was it?"

"No," he admitted.

"In fact, when we first started, you told us that she had tripped and hurt herself, didn't you?"

"I don't remember that."

"Your Honor, I'd like to read from the deposition of William Collins—"

"That was when the criminal proceeding was still going on!" Bill cut in. "I was told not to say anything about the accident!"

Judge Griffen peered over his glasses at each of us. "Criminal proceeding?"

"Yes, Your Honor," I replied. "I was not able to introduce it because of other rules of evidence, but since Mr. Collins has brought it up, may I proceed?"

The judge nodded and I turned back to Bill. "Mr. Collins, didn't you get charged with two felonies in connection with domestic violence?"

Bill went pale with the realization of his blunder. He turned to the judge. "My attorney said we couldn't talk about that in this proceeding because I got nolo something."

"Apparently something happened that prevented the plaintiff from bringing it into evidence," Judge Griffen answered. "But once you mentioned it, they can make inquiries. You may proceed, Mr. Gregory."

"Thank you, Your Honor. So, Mr. Collins, you were charged with two felonies, is that correct?"

"I guess so, I don't really remember much about that part."

"But you wound up striking a deal with the DA where you pleaded no contest to a single misdemeanor?"

"Yes."

"Do you recall what your sentence was?"

"Three months in county jail and two years probation."

"Have you served that sentence?"

"No."

"Why not? Wasn't it supposed to start last December 28th?"

"Yeah, it was. But my attorney talked to someone and it got reduced to straight probation. I think there was something about me paying support, crowding in the jails, and the holiday season. I'm not sure of all the details."

"So, just to be clear, you have gone from having two felonies charged for what you did to Carol to probation and no jail time?"

"Well, I did spend the night in jail when I was arrested."

I turned to the judge. "Your Honor, I would like to proceed with other witnesses at this time and reserve my right to recall Mr. Collins later for other matters."

Judge Griffen nodded to me. I asked Bill to stand down and go back to his seat at the table. I then called for Diane to take the stand.

50 - Dr. Gold's Testimony

May 21, 1986

Looking taller than she really was, with her power suit and including two-inch heels, Diane walked purposefully to the witness box and took a seat. I had her recite the long list of credentials and asked the judge to qualify her as an expert, which he did.

"Dr. Gold, have you formed an opinion as to the relationship between Bill and Carol?"

"Yes," she said.

"And have you formed an opinion as to how Carol's physical injuries were sustained?"

"Yes."

"And have you formed an opinion on Carol's mental and emotional injuries?"

"Yes."

I next led her through the various documents she'd reviewed to form those opinions. This was, of course, all theater to get reports into evidence that would have otherwise been hearsay. I didn't want to have the judge helping Bill preserve evidentiary niceties because Bill wasn't equipped with knowledge of evidence. I wanted to be as clean as I could with the evidence to keep the judge on our side and not bully Bill. That complete, we were set to start the real business of her testimony.

"Dr. Gold, have you been able to also form an opinion as to whether Carol Collins was the victim of domestic violence?"

"Yes. She was. She suffered systematic and ongoing domestic violence from the time of their honeymoon in March 1983 and culminating with the attack February 9, 1985."

"Why didn't she leave?" This was the question prepared so Diane could give a short course on DV.

"Victims of domestic violence—DV—don't leave for a variety of reasons. First, they believe they have no place to go and no money to get there. Their essential support system—parents, relatives—have been alienated by the perpetrator to the point they have also cut ties with the victim. She doesn't even have control of enough money to escape. Second, the victim's sense of self-worth has been diminished to the point that they may believe nobody else would have them, or worse, that they deserve what is happening to them. Third, especially when children are involved, they may believe staying and enduring what has been happening to them somehow protects their child. Fourth, once they endure the actual explosion of violence, the perpetrator usually begins an extravagant courting behavior that the victim enjoys. In some cases, the victim even instigates an event so the courting—flowers, candy, gifts, dinners out—will begin again.

"Typically that courting behavior leads him to feel diminished, having lost his power and control over the victim. In order to restore that power, he reverts to his own coping mechanism of violence and the cycle begins again. And again. And again. It's all about the perpetrator's need to be one-up and in control. Physical harm increases, sometimes including death. That is a reason police view 911 DV calls as a nightmare: the risk extends to them as well."

"Thank you for that explanation, Doctor," I said. "Do you have an opinion as to what happened between Bill and Carol?"

"Let me give you the history I've been able to piece together. When Carol first came to see me, she was ashamed and unable to speak about what had happened to her between the time of their marriage in March 1983, and the attack 23 months later in February 1985. She and Bill had been dating since, I think, August of 1982. Bill had been very charming and solicitous during that period. She became pregnant in December of 1982, they married in March of 1983 and honeymooned in Disneyland. It was on their honeymoon that Bill was first violent toward Carol, raping her after a long day in the park. In classic abuser form, the next day he was apologetic and treated her like a princess for months.

"When they returned to San Jose, they settled into a nice routine until after Joey was born that August. Carol faced all the new mother issues: sleepless nights, exhaustion, the competition between her mother and Bill's mother. Bill was able to discredit Carol's mother and drive a wedge between the mother and daughter. Bill would go out with his friends, usually on a Friday or Saturday night, and come home after two in the morning and want to have sex. Drunk and horny is a bad combination to inflict on an exhausted new mother. By history, on these occasions, Bill was not interested in foreplay, so Carol would not be in the mood when Bill was ready to begin, and he would hurt her in the process of initiating intercourse. This seemed, to Carol, to excite him more. She came to expect these hurtful acts whenever he went out drinking with his friends. But she had nowhere to turn. She also knew that he would be contrite and apologetic the next morning, promising never to hurt her again, so there would be a period of good behavior before the next act. In fact, they would generally have loving sex several times before there would be another instance of rape.

He began to bully her in other ways, including telling her his perceived sense of her inadequacy as a mother, further destroying her sense of self-worth. Carol had been overwhelmed psychologically and physically, with nowhere to turn, leaving her vulnerable to the next attack.

"Abusers have almost always been abused in some way themselves. While they feign contrition, they rarely actually feel it. There is some research that explains, because of their own childhood trauma, abusers have learned to suppress empathy or have suffered damage to the areas of the brain that control emotional impulses. So, by February of last year, Bill believed that having sex with Carol whenever and however he wanted was his right as her husband, and her pain was exciting for him."

I stopped her with a slight hand gesture. "But you haven't interviewed or treated Bill, have you? So how can you make that statement?"

"I admit that I haven't had the opportunity to interview Bill," she said, tipping her head in Bill's direction. Then she looked at the judge and continued, "I have been through this in many other cases. I believe Carol has been truthful in her sessions with me and the pattern that emerged is virtually textbook. I believe lawyers would call this Black-letter law, so I'm comfortable describing the situation. It is possible that there is another explanation, but at this point, I'm confident that this explanation is, by far, the most probable."

I let that sink in for a minute. Judge Griffen had been attentive and had taken pages of notes. I asked, "Have you read the deposition of Michelle Barnes?"

"I have," she said. She looked at the judge. "Michelle Barnes was Bill's girlfriend before he began dating Carol and they took up again after Bill and Carol separated."

The judge looked at me and asked, "Why is this relevant or important?"

I tried to contain a smile. "That was my next question for the witness, your honor," and looked at Diane.

"Because," she said, "Michelle Barnes confirms Bill's pattern of behavior—abuse—in relationships. Michelle, in her deposition, tells us how Bill gets sexually excited when he causes her pain. While her answers at deposition sound like she seems to accept the pain, she doesn't recognize or understand the risk she is in from Bill."

"What risk is that?"

"He doesn't have normal filters. His history with these two women informs me that before his story is fully told, Bill is going to seriously hurt someone again. He almost made Carol a quadriplegic. Without intervention he may develop the capacity to kill. He isolated Carol from her community of support, made her financially dependent on him, and gradually increased the pain he caused her. This is a recipe for extreme danger, including Michelle."

"Do you think Bill was genuinely contrite during the wooing phases you described?"

"No. The way both Carol and Michelle described things, the cycles between explosions—the time between acts of violence—was shortening. It was going down from months to weeks. If Bill were genuinely contrite, he would have sought help and the times would have been lengthening. It is a failure of our system that the criminal proceedings did not impose a real sentence and terms of probation that included anger management classes and therapy. I have found that, when abusers want to get better, they will help their victims re-establish healthy relationships with their families. They will enroll in anger management classes or seek individual counseling on their own. There are no indications that that was the case here."

"How can you tell that the crushing of two vertebrae in Carol's neck was not accidental?"

"There are several factors. The first was Bill's behavior immediately afterwards when he ran after her and was screaming at Jill and Tony's house. The second is found in the report of the surgeon, Dr. Anton, describing the incredible force necessary to create the kind of damage he found. You'll note, on page three of the report, his statement that Carol must have been in severe pain from the forces on her neck before the actual fractures took place. All of this tells me there was an actual intent to harm, even if the *specific* harm was not intended. This is borne out by the deposition of Michelle Barnes and what Carol has told me."

"Does that mean it is your opinion that he intended to hurt her, even if he didn't intend to break her neck?" I asked.

"Exactly."

"How has this most recent injury and the history of violence affected Carol?"

"The violent acts from March '83 to February '85 have done extreme damage to her ability to function in the world. Her ability to get or hold a job is compromised due to her lack of self-esteem. As the story of ongoing violence came out, her relationship with Jill and Tony D'Souza was damaged. They couldn't believe she'd stayed with Bill and endured that relationship without trusting them to help her. The most recent physical damage limited her ability to care for and increase her bond with her toddler, Joey. She was unable to physically care for him. She couldn't even pick him up to put him on a changing table and change his diaper, let alone comfort him or chase after him. Just wearing that halo device for eight weeks was a constant reminder of her perceived deficiencies. These injuries, as you'll see in Dr. Anton's report, often result in debilitating headaches. The average woman's head weighs about 14 pounds, the same as a bowling ball. So, think of holding your forearm perpendicular to the floor, balancing a bowling ball. The weaker your wrist, the more difficulty you will have balancing the ball for any length of time, and the more tired it will become.

"So, Carol had to do extensive exercise—physical therapy—to regain flexibility and strengthen her neck. She had to endure severe headaches. Working and caring for children generally gives purpose to women's lives. Carol has only recently been physically and emotionally capable of truly caring for Joey and going back to work. She still has a limited work schedule, there are limits on her lifting, and she still has headaches. She is unlikely to ever overcome the income progressions: that is, the career opportunities for advancement and raises that have been lost over the last year.

"In addition, Carol's ability to have a normal emotional and sexual relationship with a man may never return. We have been working on that and expect to do so for some time to come."

"Do you have an estimate as to how much more time Carol will have to spend in therapy?" I asked.

"It could be another six to eight months with weekly and group therapy. Then episodically for the rest of her life."

"Do you have an estimated cost for this program?"

"I had to laugh when you first asked that question to prepare for today. The range is too great to predict with any confidence."

"But is there a range?"

"Yes. A minimum of $10,000 over the next year for weekly private sessions and group sessions, then who knows? It will depend on her. There may be episodes when she starts to date. We will have to work on her recognition of behaviors that could lead to her winding up with another Bill. Learning how to set boundaries. Learning how to restore and maintain a relationship with Joey. It is not going to be easy for her."

I glanced at my watch. It was now 11 o'clock. We'd been at it since 9:30 without a break. Judge Griffen asked if I was done with the witness. I said yes. As a courtesy, he asked Bill how long he expected to be questioning Dr. Gold.

"I only have one question for her, Your Honor."

"Ask your question," he replied.

"Dr. Gold, you and I have never met, before today, have we?" Bill asked, half-standing.

"No."

"So what qualifies you to say who I am and what is in my mind?"

She looked him directly in the face, not at all cowed by his smarminess. "I've read your deposition, the medical records, my sessions with your ex-wife, and 25 years of experience dealing with cases like this. For instance, in your deposition, you denied that she had cried or given any indication that she was in pain.

That is directly contrary to her statements and the opinion of the surgeon that she would have been in severe pain."

Bill sank back into his seat, seemingly at a total loss as to how to deal with Diane. His cheeks had flushed to a deep red from the chastisement Diane had inflicted on him, his acne scars standing out in stark contrast to his otherwise tanned face.

"Anything further, Mr. Collins?" the judge asked.

"No, Your Honor."

"Mr. Gregory, do you have another witness?"

"Yes, Your Honor. I suggest we take a break and then I'd like to put Carol Collins on the stand."

51 - Carol's Testimony

May 21, 1986

Marty had come to court to provide another supportive presence for Carol. He took a seat beside Arnold, and I knew my partner well enough to guess that his low murmur contained reassurances that Carol would do fine. Arnold nodded and tried to give Carol a smile. It seemed more like a grimace, but she smiled back. Diane had been conflicted about whether to have Arnold in court when Carol would be talking about the specifics of the abuse she'd suffered, especially the sexual aspects. Carol told us she could do it, and that it would be easier with her father than her mother.

Carol walked weak-kneed to the witness box, the rubber stress ball Diane had given her clenched firmly in her hand, but sat resolute once she lowered herself into the witness chair. I stood by the rail of the jury box so she could look my way and not have Bill in her peripheral vision. I knew Judge Griffen had already made up his mind, but he needed to hear from her and, most importantly, she needed to be heard. We'd practiced the topics as much as we could to keep her from sounding totally rehearsed.

"How are you feeling today, Carol?" I began.

"OK, I guess. Nervous." Her voice was shaky.

"That is to be expected. Are you ready to go forward?"

"Yes."

"Where are you living?"

"With my mom and dad, in Almaden."

"Is your son with you there?"

"Some of the time."

"How is he doing when he is with you?"

"He is starting to relax." As she said this, she visibly started to relax herself.

"How is his potty training going?"

"Well, he is more than two and a half years old now, and we think he should be doing better. But he will use the training potty if reminded at regular times."

"So you still have to change him during the day?"

"Yes."

"Can you do that by yourself?"

"If I have to. We have a stepstool near the change table so I can hold his hand while he climbs up partway, then I don't have to lift him too far."

"Where does he sleep at night?"

"In a crib in another bedroom at my parents'. I am in my old room."

"Are you working at all?"

"Yes. I'm running the cash register at the Big 5 on Blossom Hill Road, four hours a day, three days a week."

"Is a full-time position available?"

"Not for me. Full-time employees have more responsibility for stocking and re-stocking. I'm not cleared for that yet. And I've started taking classes at West Valley Junior College again."

"What kind of classes?"

"For business. Accounting, marketing. And a class in Microsoft Excel."

"Are you dating?"

"I think it will be a long time before that happens." She grimaced.

"What are you doing for day care?"

"My mom helps one day a week. And my friend Jill helps out a couple of times a week. She has a son a couple of months older than Joey, so I can drop Joey off at her house while I'm at work. Because it's regular, I pay her half of my hourly pay. I get $3.50 an hour and I pay her $1.75."

"How is your relationship with your mother?"

"It's still strained, but improving. She has come with me to a session with Dr. Gold. I think it helped mom to understand the situation I was in."

I picked up the two eight-by-ten-inch photos of her wearing the halo. I'd told her she would have to identify them, but hadn't yet shown her the actual pictures: I wanted the judge to see her visceral reaction. Jules had captured all of her embarrassment and discomfort.

"Do these pictures accurately reflect you wearing the halo on March 27, 1985?"

Her eyes widened when she saw them for the first time since they were taken. She started to sob and squeezed the stress ball rapidly. She sniffed and wiped her nose with her palm. "Yes."

Carol's reaction was exactly what we'd hoped for. I shot a glance at the judge. He was leaning forward, a sympathetic expression on his face.

"How long were you in the halo?" I asked.

"Eight weeks. But it felt longer." Carol glared at Bill.

"What was it like for you to have to wear the halo?"

"My mother had to wash my hair twice a week, like I'm a two-year-old child. She gave me sponge baths. It was a little better when my Dad put on one of those hoses with a spray at the end. But I wasn't supposed to get the fleece wet. I couldn't wear anything that didn't open in the front. I couldn't wear anything between the fleece and my skin. And eating! Try eating when you are stuck looking straight ahead without looking down! It's hard even to drink without a straw. Forget soup. I needed a clean bib every meal. I felt so helpless. The first week in the halo...my arms and shoulders were black and blue from walking into doorways. I was always sleepy and spent most of my time in a recliner, even at night. You can probably tell I was hard to live with for everybody."

"Do you have any scars resulting from your injuries?"

"Yes. There is a large scar down the back of my neck which is usually covered by my hair, so I don't wear my hair up any more. There are these two smaller scars on my face." She pointed to the areas on her temples that had matching red marks. "And two more scars above and behind my ears." Again she pointed.

I asked her to stand and show the scars on her temples to the judge. When she sat back down, I asked, "Will those scars ever go away?" Facial scars, especially on a young woman, generally meant a larger award of general damages.

"I don't think so. Not completely. It's been over a year already. I think I'll be explaining them for the rest of my life." Her voice had faded to a whisper. Judge Griffen asked her to speak up.

I continued. "What was it like wearing the halo and caring for Joey?"

"If Joey would call me, I'd have to turn my whole body to see him. And he was always running into me from the side, so I wouldn't see him until he'd almost knocked me over. Whenever he ran into me, it jolted my neck and I got headaches a lot."

"Are you still having headaches?"

"Yes. Not every day, but a couple of times a week. Maybe three to four times."

"What happens when you get a headache?"

"My head starts to hurt right behind my eyes. And my eyes burn. Last year I had to take some prescription medication, but now I can take a couple of Tylenol and lie down for a while."

"Were you able to pick up Joey while wearing the halo?"

"No. And he didn't take that well. It was all I could do to sit on the couch and have him come to me there to comfort him."

"Were you able to take off the halo at all during that first eight weeks?"

"No. I forgot to tell you about getting dressed. When you can barely even see your feet, it's hard to put on socks. And forget pants. Or pulling a sweatshirt over your head."

"And after eight weeks?"

"The doctor took off the halo and had me in a foam collar that fastened with Velcro. I was allowed to take it off to shower, but I still had to wear it for activities and at night in bed."

"Do you remember what Dr. Anton said about your actual injury?"

"I think he said I'd had a torn ligament or something at the back of my neck and that the front of two of my vertebrae were partially crushed and that some pieces of bone were pushing against the sac that holds my spinal cord. He said that I was very close to losing the use of my arms and legs. That I would probably not ever be fully recovered. I'll probably have arthritis in my neck before I'm 50. I was just lucky to have the use of my arms and legs. I may have to have some discs removed. And he said something about maybe needing a fusion in my neck sometime down the road."

"And now?"

"I still have trouble turning my head or bending my neck forward. By the time I get home tonight, I'll have a headache, my neck will hurt and I'll probably have tingling in my arms and hands, legs and feet. Sometimes my eyes get blurry. It could be that way for the rest of my life."

"Dr. Gold testified to you having been raped multiple times by Bill. I believe she said the first time was on your honeymoon. Will you tell us about that experience? Even though Dr. Gold talked about it, I think the judge should hear about it from you."

"Um...OK." She flushed and took a quick look at her father, who was glaring at Bill. She started kneading the stress ball again, a sign that she was highly nervous. "I think I was about four months pregnant. We'd been racing around Disneyland all day and I was beat. We went back to our hotel after watching the fireworks. I laid down on the bed and Bill came over and started to climb on me. I said, 'Please, Bill. Not now. I'm really tired and cranky. I need to rest.' Then he said, 'Yes now. Right now. Or I'll punch the baby.' I was dehydrated and very dry...down there. He didn't care. I cried the whole time."

"What happened next?"

"He let me wash and go to sleep."

"How did Bill act toward you the next day?"

"He was very loving and nice. He apologized for hurting me earlier."

"This was in March 1983. Did he force himself on you again?"

"Yes. Joey was born that August. It was about a month after. We'd had sex a couple of times, but one night in late September, Bill had gone out with his buddies to watch a football game in some sports bar. I'd gone to sleep. He came in about 2:15 or so and wanted to have sex. He just climbed on me. I said, 'Please, no. I'm exhausted and trying to sleep. Let's do it in the morning.' He said, 'No, let's do it now.' and forced my legs apart. I couldn't fight him. I cried the whole time. Again." She had been talking softer and softer as she answered. The judge was leaning forward to hear her. The stress ball was getting a workout.

Judge Griffen asked her again to please speak up.

"Did his approach ever change?" I asked.

"Sometimes he would be very loving and try to help me, um, have a good time, too. But it seemed like every couple of months he'd want to force me."

"Other than forcing your legs apart, did he do anything else to hurt you?"

"Well, after that time in September, I started keeping some lube in the drawer next to my bed. When he'd start climbing on me, he'd let me use the lube. Then he started twisting my arms behind me or pulling my hair until I started to cry. I think that got him excited. Sometimes he'd punch me in the ribs."

She paused. "And there was the time he slammed the car door on my hand. That had me in a brace for four or five weeks."

"Do you know how many times Bill actually hurt you this way?" I asked. "I mean as part of his sexual enjoyment."

"I've tried not to think about it, but you said you wanted an estimate. My best estimate is between fifteen and twenty times before he finally broke my neck."

"Had he ever put you in a full-Nelson hold before?"

"Once, a couple of months before. We were playing Charades with my friend Jill and her husband, Tony. He wanted to act out some kind of clue about a wrestler and put me in that hold."

"Did he hurt you then?"

"Not really. I told him to stop. When he didn't stop right away, Tony started to get up from the couch. Bill stopped."

"Did Tony threaten Bill?"

"Not that I heard."

It was now a few minutes after noon. Judge Griffen asked how much longer I'd be with Carol. I said we'd need a few more minutes and we had to get the exhibits in order, so he called for a lunch break and had us come back at 1:30 p.m. Carol, Diane, Marty, and I returned to our conference room for lunch and to talk about the morning. Sue had brought up sandwiches from the deli downstairs. Diane and I both reinforced what a great job Carol had done on the stand. I asked Diane about Judge Griffen's reactions during Carol's testimony. She said he was right there with us the whole way. It helped that nobody was making objections and disrupting Carol's train of thought. When I asked her about Bill, she said he made a few notes, but mostly sat there with his head down. He couldn't even look at her when she was talking about the multiple rapes. Marty reinforced Diane's observations about the judge.

Sue and Jules joined the rest of us as we went back to court for the finale.

With Carol on the stand, she identified all the medical bills she'd received and a spreadsheet I'd prepared to detail her lost wages and other incidental expenses. All these documents were marked and accepted into evidence.

"The plaintiff rests," I told the judge, feeling the full weight of the long, tortured months leading up to that statement.

Judge Griffen asked Bill if he wanted to question the witness, and Bill replied he had a few questions.

Bill rose to his feet. "If you thought I was raping you, why didn't you say something?"

"Don't you remember me telling you to stop? Yelling at you to stop? That you were hurting me?"

"I thought you liked it that way."

"You were so anxious to get into me you never listened," Carol said. "Why did you think I was crying?"

"I thought those were tears of joy," he replied.

"Then you are a damn fool!" She forcefully spat it out at him.

The judge reared back in his chair from the strength of her response. Diane leaned over the bar to whisper to me, "No matter what, this was her chance to be strong for herself and face Bill in a safe place!"

"No more questions," Bill said, but stayed on his feet.

52 - Bill Takes the Stand

May 21, 1986

"Do you have any witnesses to call?" Judge Griffen asked Bill.

"No, Your Honor. Just myself. I'd like to testify." The judge directed him to the witness stand, reminded him that he was still under oath, and had him sit.

Bill took a deep breath. "Your Honor, I honestly believed that that was how Carol wanted to have sex," he said. "I never meant to hurt her and I'm sorry that I did. That's all I have to say."

He moved to get down from the stand, but I was already on my feet.

The judge held up his hand. "I think Mr. Gregory has a few more questions for you, Mr. Collins."

"That's right, Your Honor," I said. "Mr. Collins, one of the things we get to do in a punitive damages case is examine you as to your assets and income. You remember that we subpoenaed you to bring your last three months' wage records?"

"Yes. I have them at the desk, over there." He looked at the judge and asked if he should get them. The judge nodded. Bill went to the counsel table and gave me a handful of stubs. I found the one that had his most recent year-to-date total on it. I had him identify the stub as his, had it marked as a Plaintiff's exhibit.

"Does this stub, which I note is dated May 16th, last Friday, accurately reflect your current year-to-date pay?" I asked Bill.

"Yes."

"What is that number?"

"$38,000."

"So you are now working for Collins construction and making approximately $100,000 per year?"

"I guess so."

"Where do you live?"

"At the house on Vistamont."

"Are you now on title again?" I knew he wasn't officially on title; we'd had another title search run the previous week.

"No."

"Do you have an agreement with your father regarding that house?"

"Not really. We've talked about me buying it at some point, but no details have been worked out."

"Does anybody live there with you?"

"You mean, besides Michelle?"

"So Michelle Barnes is still living with you?"

"Yes. And sometimes Joey."

"When did you move back into that house?"

"Sometime in January."

"At the time we settled the divorce case, December 12th, were you still living with Michelle in her apartment?"

"Yes."

"And you still weren't working?"

"That's right."

"After you and Carol separated you left the Vistamont house?"

"Yes."

"Had you ever been on the title to the Vistamont house?"

"Yes."

"After you and Carol separated, is it true your father had you take your name off of the title?"

"Yes."

"And you owed your father a lot of money?"

"Yes, so what?"

I showed him the ledger his father had given us at his deposition. He identified it as such, and I had it entered into evidence. I asked him, "Have you repaid any of the money this ledger says you owe him?"

"No."

"Have you worked out an arrangement with him for repayment?"

"Only that we'll talk when all of this..." he paused and motioned around the courtroom, "is over."

"Is your father still the owner and operator of Collins Construction?"

"Yes."

"Is your brother also employed at Collins Construction?"

"Yes."

"How much is he being paid a year?"

"What difference does that make? I don't think that is relevant!"

I looked at the judge. "Collins Construction is a huge company. I believe Mr. Collins' brother is their chief financial officer and makes a substantial amount of money. Further, I believe that there is a history of manipulating the compensation to Mr. William Collins to artificially depress the amount he was required to pay in support. I believe all of this is relevant to this Court's evaluation of William Collins' ability to pay general damages and punitive damages."

"I agree." Judge Griffen turned to Bill and directed him to answer.

I repeated the question and Bill responded, "I think Robert makes something like $250,000 per year."

"Do you remember that when we first went to court you had lost your job at Collins Construction?"

"Yes."

"And that when we settled the divorce case, you were employed there again, making $30,000 per year?"

"Yes."

"And now you are making $100,000 per year?"

"Yes, about that."

"When Carol moved into the Vistamont house with you, weren't you on the title to that house?"

"Yes."

"And sometime after you and Carol separated, and the time we went to court, your name had been taken off of the title?"

"Yes."

At that point, I said I had no more questions of Bill. I didn't think the memo Michelle had kept of the money he owed her would make any difference.

Bill stepped down and told the judge he didn't have any more witnesses.

53 - Closing Arguments

May 21, 1986

Judge Griffen asked if I was ready to make a closing argument. He cautioned me that it was only a one-day trial and everything was already fresh in his mind. That was code for, "Don't do anything stupid. You've won, just tell me what you want."

So I did. "Your Honor, as far as the injury case goes, I'm not going to retrace the testimony concerning liability and the egregious nature of the defendant's conduct. I'd like to just put a few things in context and make some suggestions regarding damages.

"First, this last testimony of Mr. Collins had to do with his ability to pay punitive damages. But it had as much to do with a fraud he perpetrated on his wife, son, and the Court itself with his dealings surrounding the divorce last year. You will see in the court file about the divorce, that he had represented he was unemployed and had no prospects, having been let go by his father's company. He'd represented that his interest in the Vistamont house, where he'd lived with Carol until February 1985, had been re-conveyed to his parents in partial satisfaction of a number of debts he'd run up with them since his separation from Carol. Those debts were itemized on the ledger sheet before you. His current testimony makes those debts a joke.

"Given all of this, plaintiff requests a judgment of $400,000 in special and compensatory damages, plus $100,000 in punitive damages."

I sat down. Judge Griffen looked at Bill, who got up, red in the face and shouted, "This is crazy. My lawyer told me the case wasn't worth more than $15,000 and it didn't pay for me to have him here for that small a case!"

The judge looked at him, stony-faced. "Do you have anything further?"

"No, Your Honor."

"Is the matter submitted?"

"Yes, Your Honor," Bill and I said simultaneously.

"I will take this matter under submission and have a decision to you within a week," the judge said. "I want to look at those exhibits again and spend some time with the file on the divorce case."

With that, we packed up our files and exited the courtroom.

54 - Coming Down

May 21, 1986

Carol was visibly relieved that the case was over. As soon as we were outside of the courthouse she asked, "Do you really think we'll get that much money, Steve?"

"Carol," I said, "Marty and I have spent a lot of time talking about how much we should ask. The problem in this case is not the amount of the judgment, but collecting on it. The cases Marty works on have either insurance companies or large businesses that can pay judgments. While Bill is currently capable of paying something, he also could leave his job again to avoid paying anything. In another one of my cases we had a judgment against a husband and would attach his wages. Whenever we did that, he'd quit the job and move to a new community. We traced him three times, even into Oregon, and attached his wages three times, and finally decided that we were spending more on additional billable hours than we were collecting. So, if I were you, I wouldn't spend any time now thinking about how to spend money that is simply theoretical. Just be happy that your perseverance through this process may give you some closure, and that this judgment will cause Bill financial and social consequences."

Diane touched her forearm, briefly. "Carol," she said, "you know we went through this trial more to give you closure than recover money. You have had your day in court. You did great, by the way. You have seen Bill humbled in court. Let's step back and look at this as closing a door on a bad period from your past and think about ways you will work to improve your career options and your relationships with Joey and your parents. It will be a bonus if you get any money from Bill."

That seemed to sober Carol. "I know. I know," she said. "But it sure would be nice to have more money to make the other stuff easier."

"Enjoy the moment. Daydream all you like," I encouraged. "We'll get our judgment in a week or two, then we'll work on a plan."

When we got back to the office Marty directed us all into the conference room and he disappeared. A few minutes later he returned, a bottle of champagne in his hand and an array of champagne glasses in front of him.

"A toast!" Marty's deep baritone echoed the relief we all felt at having made it this far. He poured for each of us, and lifted his glass.

"Usually," Marty explained, "we don't do this until we get a significant award or settlement check. This case is different. All of us here in the office, plus Dr. Gold, know how much of an effort this has been for you, Carol, and for you, Steve. Let's savor it now!"

Carol looked at us all and tears came to her eyes. "Thank you." She barely choked out the words. "All of you."

Her dad shook my hand, again. There were tears in his eyes as well. "I had no idea," he whispered. "Thank you."

* * * * *

It only took two weeks to get a letter from Charles Griffen on his office letterhead. It was addressed to us as attorneys for

Carol, and to Bill as his own attorney. He had awarded the $400,000 in special and compensatory damages, plus $100,000 in punitive damages. He directed us to prepare the judgment for his signature and filing.

55 - Judgment

Harris hadn't asked anything during the length of the trial. "So," he asked, "did you get the money and everybody lived happily ever after?"

"Wouldn't that have been nice!" I laughed. "When we got the judgment, the first thing we did was have it recorded in Santa Clara County. That means that whenever Bill's name came up on a title search for real estate, the judgment would show as an unpaid lien against him. That is one of the first steps you take when doing collections. And the reason why the punitive damages award was so important was that it meant the award could not be discharged in a bankruptcy proceeding."

"It is just so frustrating," Harris commented, "that nothing bad seemed to happen to Bill."

Sarah had joined us by this time. "No kidding," she said. "There were times your grandpa was ready to explode, not just from this case. I was grateful that Marty could help him work off his anger better than I could. At least he didn't turn to alcohol like some of the attorneys we know do. Let's just say that it was one more reason to be glad Marty is part of our family. But the story isn't over yet." She looked at me with an expectant expression.

Harris held up his hand to stop me before I started. He stared at me a long while, frowning, then turned toward Sarah. "It sounds like Grandpa Steve wasn't much fun to be around while this case was going on. Was he?"

Sarah laughed. "We worked it out. When he came home too stressed out to be nice, I'd tell him to go for a run or call Marty. Or both. That was code for him to get his act together and not take his frustrations out on the family. That settled him down— in a hurry. I don't think he would have been any different if he'd been in any other profession; that is who he is, the man I married. I have friends who deal with stuff that makes them crazy, too. I haven't worked full time in a long time, but my women friends that work complain about all the crazy stuff they have to deal with on the job, with the added complications from sexist behaviors by their supervisors and even their subordinates. The important thing is to be doing something that you like, and not just to put food on the table."

She gave me one of her sweet smiles. I leaned over and planted a kiss on her cheek, grateful as always for her understanding, unconditional support.

"About six months after the lien was recorded," I said, "we brought Bill back to Family Court, seeking an increase in child and spousal support. That means we could get information about his current assets and income. Judge DePalma increased both. Bill refused to pay the increased amount and DePalma held him in contempt, putting him in county jail until the money was paid."

"How long did that take?" Harris asked.

"The contempt hearing was on a Friday afternoon. Those days, the banks weren't open on Saturday and we weren't going to take anything less than a certified check. That meant that Bill would stay in jail until the judge ordered his release, and the judge wouldn't order the release until he heard from me. It took until late Monday morning for Thomas to have the check delivered, since I'd asked that it be a certified check only from my bank in the office building—if he wanted it to be done as quickly as possible. I took it downstairs and deposited it. I knew the bank manager. She assured me it was all good and I called DePalma's clerk. The judge was already at lunch and got around to notifying the Sheriff's office sometime that afternoon."

"Bill spent a long weekend in jail? That's all?" Harris shook his head.

"Sometime I'll have to take you on a field trip to the county jail." I smiled, then continued. "I think the rest of his family put some pressure on Bill. So, Bill paid the arrears and the increased support, plus my attorneys' fees. Plus, you remember that Dr. Gold said she expected to continue to work with Carol?"

"Yes," Harris said. "Did she get any better?" He sounded genuinely concerned for Carol.

"Yes, she did. Part of it was that Joey was getting older, but a lot had to do with her father being at the trial and hearing what Dr. Gold said in her testimony. That gave Arnold something to take home to Arlene, Carol's mother, in a way that Carol couldn't do herself. Not that Arlene ever became warm and fuzzy, but it allowed them as parents and grandparents to work out signals to help Carol and Joey. It also opened them up to giving Carol more support—financial as well as emotional—to move into an apartment of her own and get back to school.

"A few years after the contempt incident, Collins Construction was bidding on a job for Santa Clara County— perhaps tens of millions of dollars. The bidding contractors all had to be bonded. As part of the bonding process, the bonding company investigated the principals of each construction company. In doing so, the judgment lien against Bill showed up and threatened to keep Collins from having a chance at the job.

I was surprised to hear from Thomas Collins, wanting to negotiate for a satisfaction of the lien.

"After a bit of back-and-forth, we got it settled. The actual lien was, in total, $500,000, plus judgment interest: 10% per year, simple interest. If I remember correctly, the total would have come to $650,000, but we settled for $575,000. Carol got $290,000 and we got $285,000, which I used for our costs and Dr. Gold's.

"By then, Carol had finished her AA degree at West Valley JC. And, with the help of Diane, had actually started dating someone who treated her with respect and caring. I think Joey was about seven when this happened. Carol couldn't leave the area without messing up the child sharing situation, but the money gave her the security to get a job and pay for day care. Diane fills me in after her periodic conversations with Carol. After a few administrative jobs, she wound up in marketing support at Apple, where she thrived, and wound up marrying a young man she met at work."

I leaned over and reached for Sarah's hand. She'd journeyed alongside me throughout this saga, every step of the way, including sharing it with our grandson.

"So, Harris, what did you think about the story?" *I asked.*

Harris gave me that shy smile. "I have a confession to make. I talked to Uncle Marty before I asked you to tell me about it. But only to get some questions to bring up. He said to be sure to ask about the 'halo' case."

I was already laughing. "Did he say why?"

"Sort of. He said this case was something of a breakthrough for you and it made you a better lawyer."

"No question. It made me more focused on helping families resolve their conflicts rather than escalating them," I said. "Now, how do you feel about a major?"

"I've already decided to study business and psychology in undergrad. I'll make up my mind about going on to grad school later. And law does sound interesting." He hesitated, looking at our joined hands, as if his question might threaten our bond. Finally he asked, "Do you ever talk to Carol?"

"No, we don't talk. But every year on May 21st, the anniversary of the trial, Carol sends Sarah a lovely flower arrangement."

Acknowledgements

If you ask anybody who knows me, you'll find out that at any given moment you could hold me upside down and shake me and ideas and words would fall out like Legos—all shapes, sizes and colors. I don't think it is idea-phoria or AHDD, but it is something that friends and colleagues recognize. Then, like any six-year-old, I put them together in a way that makes sense to me and announce, "I've built a car!" Then other people come along and gently move some of the pieces around to make the final product recognizable.

Writing this book is something like that car. First it was my wife, Barbara, telling me to put the wheels on the bottom. At an early stage, Myra Slatoff told me she wanted to read more of the story. Patty Flores Reinhart talked to me about my characters. Nancy Ross, LCSW, and Keith Britany, MFT, helped me with the psychology—naming the dynamics and behaviors of the principal characters.

Steve Green, MD, helped me conceptualize the telling of the story by having a later discussion with a friend. I then came up with a conversation with my grandson. Steve also connected me with Jeff Englander, MD, who corrected some of the medical aspects of Carol's surgery and recovery and loaned me a halo that the doctors at Santa Clara County Medical Center currently use for teaching.

The cover could not have been done without graphic artist Sue Bialson, creating an image with real impact.

Thanks also to my granddaughter, Ashley, for being a good sport in putting on a halo to pose for the cover picture.

A special thank you goes out to Author Ann Bridges, who, as editor and publisher, guided me through the process of bringing this story to press. Without her, that Lego car would have never made it out of second gear.

Author's Note

Have you ever had an itch you couldn't scratch? Watch someone with a cast on their arm or leg trying to get to that itch with a backscratcher? *The Girl in the Halo* was born of that itch. The character, Carol, is the composite of many different women I met during my 48 years practicing law. The context—*recovering civil damages despite myriad hurdles imposed by the system*—was the itch. As I approached retirement, looking back on all the cases I'd worked on, this segment of my practice stood out as needing a good scratch, hence "my most memorable case."

Writing an article for a journal wasn't going to scratch that itch. Been there, done that. I've even done presentations for professional organizations to help professionals (lawyers, therapists, financial advisors) recognize their need to advise their clients about the pursuit of damages for abuse they have suffered. Financial abuse of spouses (and elders) is rampant. A little-known detail is that the outcry for a broader definition of spousal abuse started with the onset of AIDS, as bringing home any kind of STD became in and of itself grounds for a domestic violence tort.

Another fact: real people don't read law journals. They do read legal fiction. Hence, the vehicle. As a lawyer, I was accustomed to writing with footnotes, endnotes, and extended parenthetical phrases. To avoid that format, I inserted Harris for a chance to explain, in a less formal way, what was happening, and try to help the reader understand the legal process.

The criminal preliminary hearing and subsequent plea bargain described in this book are also disturbingly similar to an experience I had in 1986: A defendant was allowed to plead no contest to a misdemeanor after having been charged with multiple felonies. The victim was never contacted after the preliminary—by the DA or the Adult Probation Department. In fact, to the best of my knowledge, the Adult Probation Department never did a report of any kind. The defendant served only three months, never had to register as a sex offender, and returned to live freely in Santa Clara County. A real failure of the justice system. If you, as a reader, are upset that Bill seemed to escape with no real-world consequences, you can share my itch. Keep reading for a way to extend that back scratcher.

An early mentor told me to watch whatever was the most popular legal show on TV because that would inform my clients. This meant that I could be screaming at the TV that the portrayal on the screen was not real. (Carol pointed that out in this novel.) So this is a book that I hope pulls back the curtain on the reality of what happens in family cases—how the sausage is made.

At the surface, the book is about just that: the process and how it grinds up anybody who dares do anything but accept that stuff flows downhill. Below the surface, I hope, the reader will get a better sense of the teams of professionals that grate their knuckles into the sausage: the lawyers, the therapists, the custody evaluators, the investigators, and their families.

I hope that this book will, in some way, bring awareness to our readers and pressure on our legislators to change elements of various California statutes to expand remedies for victims. In fact, I have written proposed statutory amendments that have, as yet, failed to capture a following among California legislators. I suspect it is because they, like the judges you met in this book, simply don't want to get into a messy area. I also suspect that when the various organizations that support victims of spousal abuse join the cause, it will wake up those legislators.

Proceeds to charity: My plan is to make sure that at least 50% of any profits will flow to charitable organizations helping victims of spousal abuse. Perhaps their voices will be heard in Sacramento.

About Alan L. Nobler

Alan grew up in the San Francisco Bay Area, earned his undergraduate degree from San Jose State University, his law degree from Santa Clara University, and then practiced law in Silicon Valley for forty-eight years. Starting before the age of specialization, he practiced divorce, personal injury, and real estate litigation; formed corporations and partnerships; wrote wills and trusts. He became a California Certified Family Law Specialist in 1980. As part of his work with divorcing families, he handled child custody, domestic violence, and restraining order litigation. His background working in personal injury cases led him to pursue domestic violence torts as depicted in *The Girl in the Halo.*

After closing his practice in 2017, Alan continues to teach and advocate for victims' rights, including shaping potential California state legislation for future consideration and debate.

For more about Alan and the charities he hopes to benefit, please visit **www.nobler.com**.

Made in the USA
Middletown, DE
21 March 2021

35387669R00158